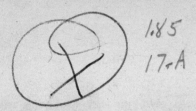

"I need someone to take that job I offered you, and I thought maybe I could convince you to take it," she said.

"How did you plan to do that?" I asked.

She sighed and shook her head at me, as if she couldn't understand me. "How do you think?"

Her hands went to the buttons on my shirt and she quickly undid them . . . .

Don't miss any of the lusty, hard-riding action in the new Charter Western series, THE GUNSMITH:

THE GUNSMITH

12

THE CANADIAN PAYROLL

J.R. ROBERTS

ACE CHARTER BOOKS, NEW YORK

THE GUNSMITH #12: THE CANADIAN PAYROLL
Copyright © 1983 by Robert J. Randisi

An Ace Charter Original

Published by arrangement with the author

ISBN: 0-441-30867-8

First Ace Charter Printing: January 1983
Published simultaneously in Canada

Manufactured in the United States of America
Ace Books, 200 Madison Avenue, New York, New York 10016

TO PETER HOM

PROLOGUE

One hundred and fifty miles south of the Canadian border, in Montana, the cold had lessened considerably. Up until this point, Assistant Commissioner Macleod and his three Northwest Mounted Police troopers had endured the dangers of a large herd of buffalo, which had nearly trampled them, and a howling blizzard, which had struck them about fifty miles from the border, inside the U.S.

James Macleod was a tall, full-bearded man in his late thirties. He had been a soldier since joining the initial Red River expedition into Metis country as a militiaman in 1870. He was of that rare breed of officer, both tough and popular, admired by his men for his ability and his sense of fair play. He had risen steadily through the ranks of the Mounties. The largest Mountie outpost along the Canadian-U.S. border had been named Fort Macleod, in his honor.

The life of a Mountie in an isolated wilderness was lonely, to say the least. For the most part, the men were able to combat the loneliness, but when it combined with six months of payless paydays, something had to give—and it did.

During the winter of 1874-75, eighteen men had

1

deserted from Fort Macleod, and Macleod himself didn't much blame them. In spite of all of his efforts they had not been paid for more than six months.

Finally, in March of this year, 1875, Macleod had been able to persuade the bureaucrats to arrange for a payroll of over thirty thousand dollars. All he had to do was ride three hundred miles south to pick up the money from a bank in Helena, Montana.

In addition to his three troopers, Macleod had taken along Jerry Potts, a short, muscular, bowlegged halfbreed who was the best damn scout and guide he knew of.

"How much farther?" he asked Potts now.

"Hell, Commissioner, we ain't but halfway there yet," Potts replied.

"Well, at least it's getting warmer," Macleod said.

"Sure," Potts said. "Can't be more than fifteen, twenty degrees now."

Macleod gave his guide a sour look, but remained silent.

They rode on in relative safety for the next hundred miles, and then, fifty miles outside of Helena, Potts pulled up and signaled for the rest of them to stop.

"What's wrong?" Macleod asked.

"Ain't sure," Potts said, rubbing his jaw. "Something just don't feel right."

"Would you care to elaborate?" Macleod asked.

"I'd love to, Commissioner, but I can't. Not yet, anyways. I just figger maybe we oughta be a little careful from here on in."

"As you wish," Macleod sighed. "May we go on now?"

"Sure, Commissioner, sure."

They hadn't ridden another hundred yards when there was a shot.

"Where'd that come from?" Macleod demanded, producing his own pistol. His men also had their guns in their hands, but he noticed that Potts's hands were empty.

"Potts," he called out.

"Put your gun up, Commissioner, and tell your men to do the same. Then just stand ready."

Macleod figured he had brought Potts along because the halfbreed knew what he was doing, so he gave the order and holstered his own gun. Presently he became aware of the sound of hoofbeats, and then about ten men suddenly appeared from behind rocks and trees, all wearing the uniform of the United States Army.

Macleod breathed a little easier, because he had expected much worse.

The border patrol appeared to be under the command of a sergeant, who rode up to Potts and Macleod.

"You men mind telling me what your business is?" the sergeant demanded.

"Would you mind asking your men to ease up on their guns, Sergeant?" Macleod countered with his customary calm. "I will show you my identification papers, if I may reach into my jacket."

"Do it slow, mister," the sergeant replied.

Macleod and his men were not clad in their red-coated Mountie uniforms because, technically, across the border they had no authority. Now Macleod produced the proper papers identifying him and his men as Northwest Mounted Police, on a special mission to Helena, Montana.

The sergeant scanned the papers and then handed them back with a thoughtful look on his face.

"I'm sorry to hold you up, sir," he said. "We thought you might have been whiskey runners."

"Quite understandable, Sergeant," Macleod replied, accepting his papers back. "You are to be commended for performing your duties so diligently."

"Thank you, sir. You and your men can go now," the sergeant said.

"Thank you, Sergeant," Macleod said. "Mr. Potts, let us continue on."

"Yes, sir, Commissioner," Potts said, keeping a wary eye on the sergeant.

As the Canadians rode on, the sergeant watched, his face still thoughtful. A corporal, his second in command, rode up by him and said, "What's the matter, Sarge?"

"I been hearing stories about a lot of money being held in the Helena bank, Starkey," he said.

"So?" the corporal asked, wondering what Sergeant Ben Cory had in mind.

"Well, I'm starting to think that maybe I know what that money's being held for," Corey said. "And I'm thinking that if we stay out here long enough, a lot of money could come riding right into our hands." Corey looked at Starkey and asked, "You'd be all for that, wouldn't you, Will?"

"I guess so, Sarge," Starkey replied.

"Yeah, well, I don't *guess* so," Corey said, looking back at the five Canadians, who were further away now.

"Let's join up with the other half of our patrol,

Starkey, and then we'll find out what all of the men think."

"Okay, Sarge," Starkey agreed.

Corey looked after the retreating backs of the five Canadians once more, and figured that the next time he saw them, they'd be bringing him a lot of money. . . .

ONE

I wasn't used to this kind of cold, and I was thinking that if this was what the Northwest was like, maybe I'd be heading south again sooner than I thought.

I came from the East when I was younger, and since then I'd spent most of my life in the Southwest. Lately, I figured it was time for me to see what the Northwest was like. And maybe my reputation wouldn't get there before me, as it had all over the South.

Before entering Montana, the farthest north I'd ever been was Wyoming. After Montana I figured on taking a look at the Dakotas, and then head back south through Nebraska.

I pulled the blanket tighter around me and thought maybe I'd be heading back through Wyoming soon.

I wondered how my horses—my team and my big black, Duke, who was following along behind—felt about the cold. Did they ever care what the weather was like? We'd seen some cold winters in Texas together, but nothing like I'd run across in Montana.

Helena, Montana was about three hundred

miles from the Canadian border, and I could just imagine what kind of weather they were having up there.

All I was hoping to find in Helena was some hot coffee, a woman who wouldn't mind sharing the warmth of her body and her bed, a hot meal, and a poker game. Not necessarily in that order.

As I rode down the main street of Helena I shucked the blanket from my shoulders and dumped it behind me into my wagon. There was no point in advertising the fact that I was more used to warmer weather than to the cold.

I got directions to the livery stable, and on the way I saw that Helena was set up just like any other mining town I'd ever been in. Saloons and gambling houses, ready and willing to take the miners' money from them. And the miners, just as willing to fill the places up and lose their money.

I put Duke, the team, and the rig up in the livery and then went looking for that cup of coffee.

The first place I passed looked like it was a general store, trading post, café and saloon all rolled into one, in a room that wouldn't hold twenty people. I wanted a cup of hot coffee much too badly to keep going, so I stopped in. There were no gambling materials in the place, which I figured accounted for its being empty, although the lady behind the counter was pretty enough to draw a crowd all by herself.

She had red hair and the palest green eyes I'd ever seen. She appeared to be about twenty-eight, with a full, womanly body that started to warm me up already. It looked like I might have come to the right place to get all of those things I was thinking about on the trail.

"Hello," I said, walking up to the counter.

"Howdy," she replied, looking up from cleaning the countertop. "What can I get you?"

"What have you got?" I asked, looking around. "I'm not quite sure what kind of a place I walked into."

Every inch of wall space was covered up with one thing or another. Shelves holding canned goods, furs, guns—you name it—she had hanging on the walls.

"I can get you a drink, a meal, supplies, just about anything you need," she said, looking me straight in the eye. I wondered if she knew what her statement was conjuring up in my mind.

"What do you call this place?"

"It's a little bit of a saloon, little bit of a general store, little bit—"

"Little bit of a place, huh?" I said.

She smiled and said, "Yes, that, too."

"Well, I'd like a hot meal if I can get one, and plenty of hot coffee."

"I can help you with the meal if you'll take beef stew," she said. "Coffee comes with it."

"Fine."

"Have a seat if you can make your way through the crowd," she said. "I'll get it right out."

I had my pick of tables since the place was empty, so I grabbed a corner one and pushed my back right up against the wall. Maybe my reputation didn't reach this far, but there was no harm in playing it safe.

I hoped the meal was decent as well as hot, because it was dinner hour and the place was still empty. There had to be a reason for that.

She came out carrying a tray with a bowl of

steaming hot stew, a loaf of bread and a pot of coffee.

"Always this slow?" I asked.

"The miners can't find a game in here," she said, "and they want that more than they want good food."

"Makes sense," I said. She waited there while I tasted the stew. It was hot and delicious, and I told her so.

"I'm glad you like it. You just get into town?" she asked.

"Yep. Just rode in, haven't even registered at a hotel yet. Your place was the first place I passed, and I needed some food and some coffee."

"You wouldn't need a job, too, would you?" she asked, hopefully.

My mouth was full, so I shook my head while I swallowed and then said, "Sorry, no."

"Damn," she said, and I looked at her. She looked disappointed, which somehow made her even prettier.

"This place doesn't look that busy that you need help," I said.

"I don't," she said, "not here."

"What's the job, then?"

"You interested?"

"I said no," I reminded her.

"Then there's no need for you to know what it is, is there?" she asked, and went back behind the bar.

TWO

Since I didn't want a job, the red-haired woman ignored me the rest of the time I was eating. When I finished the food and the coffee, I asked if I could have a cold beer, and she brought it over without a word and set it down in front of me. As she started clearing my table, I said, "That was a mighty fine meal, miss."

"Thanks," she said.

I sipped the beer and said, "Beer's cold, too."

"That ain't so hard, with the kind of weather we have here," she pointed out. That struck me as an immediate advantage that the Northwest had over the Southwest: Getting cold beer would be no problem. Still, the disadvantages outweighed what advantages I had seen so far.

The cold beer covered the warm food and coffee very nicely, and there was a comfortable glow inside of my stomach. I took one look out the window and dreaded going out into a blowing wind and possible snow.

"Looks like it might snow," I said.

"It will," she said. "You aren't from around here, are you, mister?" she asked, showing the first signs of interest since I had turned down her job.

"Is that obvious?" I asked.

"You got a tan, and your clothes don't exactly fit the climate," she said.

"You can say that again," I replied, remembering how the cold wind had cut right through my clothes.

"If you're planning on staying around, you better outfit yourself with some heavier clothes."

"You wouldn't happen to have any around, would you?" I asked.

"Just so happens I would."

"I thought so."

I followed her to the counter and bought a few heavy shirts, a new pair of boots, and a couple of new pairs of britches, all of which were designed to keep the wind off your flesh.

"Well, it seems you've just about given me everything I need," I said to her, looking her straight in the eye. She held my gaze for a moment, then let a bored expression come over her face and went back to cleaning the countertop.

"Well, I'm much obliged," I said, starting for the door.

"Come back when you get hungry again," she said, "or if you decide you need a job."

"I'll keep it in mind," I promised. "Where is the nearest hotel?"

"You want the closest, or the best?" she asked.

Thinking about the cold I said, "Better make it the closest."

"Just go outside, make a right and walk to the end of the block. That's the closest one."

"Again, much obliged," I said.

"Don't thank me until you see the hotel," she advised.

"Okay. I'll see you again."

She didn't reply, so I opened the door and went out into the cold again, very curious about her entire operation. As soon as the cold cut through my clothing, though, I forgot about her and concentrated on just finding shelter.

I followed her instructions and found myself standing in front of a small, somewhat rundown building with the letters H TEL above the door. I was too cold to be running around town being choosy about where I stayed, so I went on in.

"Can I get a room?" I asked the clerk, a bored, scruffy-looking man in his forties. He looked surprised.

"Sure, mister," he said, almost falling as he hopped down off his stool and approached the desk. "Jest sign the register."

"Can I have a room overlooking the front street?" I asked.

"Mister, you can just about have any room in the place that you want," he said.

"Just one overlooking the street," I said.

"That's fine," he said. He turned the register around and looked at my name and his face showed no recognition at all. "All right, Mr. Adams," he said, reaching behind him for a key. "You can have room number ten." He handed me the key and said, "It overlooks the street and you have a clear view of Miss Lottie's Pleasure Palace."

"Is that a fact?" I said, taking the key. "Well, I always say there's nothing like a room with a view."

"Ain't that the truth," he agreed.

I took my key, my saddlebags, and my rifle and went up the rickety staircase, hoping that it would hold me.

When I got to my room there was no need to use the key because the door was wide open. The room was small and dusty, but the bed was made, so I didn't think anyone had used it very recently.

It wasn't the bridal suite, but as I looked out the window I saw that I did indeed have a view of Miss Lottie's Pleasure Palace.

THREE

There were no bath facilities in my "h tel," and I probably would have froze my ass off if I tried to take one. As it was, washing myself from a wash-basin was a bone-chilling experience, and I dressed quickly in my new, heavier clothing. I checked the door to make sure the lock worked and then, properly insulated from the cold by my new clothing, I left the hotel in search of a saloon, and a poker game.

Outside the cold bit at my face and made my eyes water, and darkness was falling. With the sun gone, the temperature was dropping even further. I followed my ears and found a well-lit saloon with music and loud voices emanating from it, and I stepped inside.

It was a large place, with some gaming tables, and a few poker games going on. The bar was crowded, and a piano player in the corner was sup-plying all of the music. There were so many people there that just their body heat was warming up the room.

I elbowed up to the bar and ordered a beer, then turned to look at the three poker tables. There were no empty chairs, so when the bartend-

14

er brought my beer I asked him, "Can anybody sit in on those games, or are they private?"

"Soon as there's an empty seat, mister, it's all yours," he said.

"Thanks," I said. I picked up my beer, then put my back to the bar to watch the tables, and pick the one I wanted to play at.

One table looked as if it were manned solely by miners. There wasn't a man in the bunch who could perform a clean shuffle. If I sat at that table, I would have cleaned up. It would have been easy, and no fun. I decided to let them play amongst themselves, so that their money would simply continue to go back and forth, and nobody would get hurt.

The second table looked like a mixture of miners and town merchants, with no professional gamblers in evidence. The situation was similar. Their money changed hands over the counter often enough, so perhaps at the end of the game, things would even out.

The third table was the one that caught my interest. There were two or three miners among the six players, but the other three men seemed to know what they were about with a deck of cards. Two of them had guns on their hips and were wearing plain trail clothes, but the third was wearing a black suit with a string tie, and I could tell that he was wearing a gun in a shoulder rig underneath his right arm. The two men with the handguns on their hips knew how to play cards, that was plain, but the man in the suit was obviously a seasoned, professional gambler.

And a cheat.

Oh, he was very good at it, but it was quite

obvious—to me, anyway—that he was using some kind of a holdout. My guess was that he was wearing a simple sleeve holdout, which would be worn on his arm and would thrust a card into his waiting hand with a simple extension of his elbow. It was the simplest one, and he probably figured that no one in a mining town like Helena would pick it up, or even look for it.

There were several different kinds of holdouts, including breastplate holdouts, a holdout vest, and the amazing Kepplinger holdout, a harness of pulleys, cords and telescoping silver-plated tubes, which reached from a man's forearm to his shoulders and down to his knees. To activate the amazing contraption, the wearer had only to spread his knees slightly and a clawed "sneak," hidden between the sleeves of a special double shirtsleeve, moved towards his hand with a card.

I was sure that if this man's gear were checked in his hotel room, more than one of these would be found, in addition to the one he was wearing now.

The other men at the table, as far as I could see, were playing fairly, and the large piles of chips in front of the gambler showed who was winning steadily.

There's one thing about cheating that makes a game interesting. If you know who is cheating, and how, you can sometimes use that against him.

I decided to do just that.

One of the miners finally tapped out, and I moved forward hurriedly to take his seat. Maybe I was playing the wrong game, but I first intended to use the man's cheating against him if I could, and failing that, I'd expose him.

"Mind if I take this chair?" I asked the players.

"Help yourself, friend," the gambler said, eagerly. "Always welcome fresh money."

"I'll bet," I said, under my breath.

The miner seated next to me apparently heard me, because he laughed and said, "You'll need cards before you can do that, friend.

"You're right," I said.

He was a pretty friendly guy, and he talked a lot during the game. If you're going to beat a cheater, you need to be able to concentrate, and that meant no talking, yet I didn't want to be rude to the man.

"What's your name, friend?" he asked.

"Adams," I said.

"Mine's Beauchamp," he said. "I'm from Canada."

I nodded and said, "Really," while I examined my first hand. One of the miners had dealt a hand of five card draw, and I had a pair of kings.

"I open," I said. "What are the stakes?"

"Small," the gambler said. "Friendly. You can open for five dollars."

"Five dollars," I said.

The friendly miner, Beauchamp, was on my left and he said, "These cards aren't kind tonight. I'll fold."

The man next to him called, and then the gambler raised me five dollars. The players between him and me hesitated, but called. I called, and so did the fifth player still in the game.

The dealer looked at me and I said, "Two," keeping my kings, and an ace kicker.

Around the table most of the men took three

cards, indicating that they might have a pair. The gambler took one. He might have had two pair, but I saw the muscle in his arm twitch, and I figured that he was filling in a straight or a flush with a holdout card.

When he looked at his card—and no one noticed the switch but me, of that I was sure—he made a clucking sound with his tongue, as if he were trying to fill in and had failed.

I bet into him, saying, "Five dollars," to see what he would do. I had not improved my hand, and still had only kings.

The one player between us on my left called, and the gambler raised me, smirking at his own private joke. He had to figure I would call.

The two players between us on my right folded, and so did I. The disappointment on the gambler's face was obvious to me, and the last player folded, leaving the gambler with a relatively small pot, one not worth the use of a holdout card.

I didn't know how many he had, but I had made him waste one. With some holdout rigs, you were able to hide an entire deck, but I didn't think that was the case here. He must have been playing for a few hours, and his holdout cards were probably dwindling. To have had to waste one here was a blow.

The deal came to me and I dealt a hand of five card stud. That would reveal to me four of his cards, leaving him only one to replace with a holdout. It would be easy to figure what his best possible hand could be.

When the cards were dealt, there were several small pairs on the table, and Beauchamp had dropped out. The gambler was sitting with a pair of kings in front of him. If he used a holdout card, he could give himself three kings. I hoped he would, because I had a pair of aces showing, with one in the hole, only I didn't bet them like I had them. I wanted him to think that all I had was a pair, so he'd use a holdout card.

I watched him carefully. There were enough men still in the game to make a holdout card worth it, and when I saw the muscle twitch, I knew he had done it. He was good, all right. If I hadn't been watching him, I never would have been able to tell that he'd pulled a switch.

I was high on the table with a pair of aces, so I bet five dollars. The gambler raised when it came his turn, sure that his three kings had my two aces beat. Two other players called his raise, which meant that they had either two pair, or a small three of a kind, neither of which was anything to worry about. The gambler and I were the power on the table with three of a kind each.

When it came to me I said, "I raise ten dollars."

The other players exchanged glances, but nobody complained. When the bet reached the gambler, he hesitated, then raised me ten. The other players dropped out after that, and I reraised him ten dollars.

"You're pretty sure of those aces," he said. "You know I've got kings showing, don't you?"

"Play them," I said.

"You're bluffing," he said.

"It's your play, mister."

"Gates is the name, Adams," he said, "and I'm going to raise you twenty. It's going to cost you to bluff."

I was glad he had raised twenty, because I came back and doubled his raise.

"Forty dollars," I said.

"There is a limit, you know," Gates said.

"You went to twenty," I reminded him. "You mean to tell me I can't go to forty?"

He stared at me, then counted out forty dollars in chips and threw it in. Almost as a last thought, he counted out fifty and said, "I raise, friend."

"I won't double it this time," I said, and he smirked, but lost his smirk when I said, "but I will match it. Raise fifty."

I threw the fifty in and his face fell. He didn't know how, but somehow he had been taken.

"Call," he said. "What have you got?"

"Trip aces," I said, flipping the ace in the hole.

"Damn," he said, throwing his hole card down. It flipped over, showing the third king.

"That was some hand, gentleman," Beauchamp said. He gathered up the cards for his deal and continued, "Do you mind if the rest of us play now?"

The other players were happy to see Gates get his comeuppance, though, and Gates knew it.

Things went bad for him after that, holdout or no holdout.

The two men in trail clothes caught on first, and everytime they dealt they played five card stud. The miners eventually caught on as well, and soon the only time the game was different was when Gates dealt five card draw. Then I would raise, even with a bum hand, until everyone else dropped out, and finally I'd drop out, leaving Gates with a small pot.

The pile of chips in front of Gates began to dwindle steadily, and soon he had less than he had sat in with.

"I think that will be all for me, gentlemen," he said, trying to hold himself together. I thought he recognized the fact that the game had changed when I sat down, and he might have been afraid that I knew what he was doing. As a professional gambler, he knew how to counter a holdout as well as I did.

He looked me in the eye as he stood up and said, "You play a good game, mister."

"Thanks," I said. I didn't return the compliment. He cashed in his chips and left the saloon, and probably town, as well.

"Well, Mr. Adams," Beauchamp said, "it looks like you really changed everyone's luck when you sat down.

"Is that so?" I said. "How did you boys do?"

"Looks to me like we all came back pretty much," Beauchamp said. We looked around the table and the others verified that they had either gotten even, or were ahead.

"You men are miners, right?" I asked, directing myself to the three unarmed men.

"That's right," Beauchamp answered for them all.

"I wouldn't expect any better from you, then, but you two," I said to the men were obviously passing through town, "I'm surprised at you. I thought you were pretty savvy poker players when I came in."

"What do you mean?" one of them demanded.

"You ought to know when a man is using a hold-

out on you," I said, and the two of them exchanged angry glances.

"You mean, that slicker was cheatin'?" one of
them demanded.

"For as long as I've been here," I said.

"Sonofabitch," the other man said from between his teeth. They both got up and made as if to
follow Gates, and I tried to stop them.

"He's long gone, gents," I said. "He knew I
spotted him."

"Why didn't you say something?" one of them
asked.

"Hey, it isn't my job to sit down and watch out
for the other players, is it? You guys are going to
play cards, you better be able to tell when somebody is cheating."

"Come on, Lou," one said to the other. "Let's
see if we can't catch that cheat."

They left anyway, looking for him and I hoped
he had gotten himself out of town, or there'd be a
killing.

When they were gone Beauchamp said, "I'm a
little lost, friend. How did you know he was cheating, and what's a holdout?"

"You want a free lesson in poker?" I asked
him.

"Hell, no," he said. "Bartender, get my friend
Mr. Adams here another beer, on me." He looked
at me and said, "I'm a little ahead, thanks to you,
so I'm buying."

"Then I'm talking."

I explained how I had spotted the man cheating and how the various gambler's holdouts
worked, and described ways they could be beat, or

at least neutralized.

"This is amazing," Beauchamp said afterward, looking at his fellow miners. "That's Robert, and that dour looking man is LeClerc," he said, introducing the other two men. "We owe you a debt of thanks, Mr. Adams, even though you do not sit down at a game to watch out for the other players. We will buy another round."

"Well," I said, "I'm much obliged."

"Would you care to continue playing?" he asked, and then added, "For considerably smaller stakes, that is."

Actually, I did not like to play for very low stakes, but I liked Beauchamp, so decided to stay and pass the time. Besides, the saloon was probably considerably warmer than my hotel room.

I found out some very interesting things from Beauchamp, who was very candid, sometimes to the annoyance of the other two men.

"Come now," he told his friends at one point, "this man saved us great financial loss, and certainly embarrassment. He should be treated with the utmost confidence."

Whether they agreed or not, Beauchamp told me their story, and a story that also applied to fifteen other men in Helena, Montana.

He said that all of them were Northwest Mounted Police who had deserted, crossing the border from Canada to Montana and coming to Helena to work the mines, because they had not been paid their salaries for the better part of six months. That combined with the loneliness and boredom of being stationed in an isolated wilderness, had caused them to make their decision.

"What about your outfit?" I asked. "Your commanding officer. Won't they send someone after you?"

"Our commander is a saint," Beauchamp said expansively. "Assistant Commissioner Macleod, for whom Fort Macleod was named, tried his best to get us paid, but it was no use. No, I don't think the commissioner even blames us for doing what we did."

With that the other two men agreed wholeheartedly, and I thought that for a commanding officer, this fella Macleod must have been a rare one.

Of course, I didn't know whether I believed the story or not, but it had been a pleasant way to spend an evening. I had drunk a lot of beer, made a few dollars—mostly at the expense of the gambler, Gates—and I had made a new friend in the miner/ex-Mountie, André Beauchamp.

"Are you leaving us?" Beauchamp asked as I rose and gathered up my chips.

"I'm afraid so. I just got to town today, and I think I need a few hours sleep."

"Are you going to be staying in town long?" he asked.

"I don't know, yet, I said, honestly. "I've got no place to go in a hurry, but I have to see what this town offers."

Beauchamp slapped me on the shoulder and said, "Meet me here tomorrow evening, and I will show you what pleasures Helena holds. Agreed?"

"Agreed," I said without hesitation. "I'll see you here tomorrow." Before leaving, though, I leaned over and said to him, "Watch who you play cards with while I'm gone, all right?"

He laughed and slapped me on the back, assuring me that they would be very careful from now on with whom they played, thanks to me.

FOUR

When I got back to my hotel the desk clerk urgently waved me over to him.

"What's the matter?" I asked.

"You have a visitor in your room, Mr. Adams," he said, "and I don't want to get blamed."

"Did you let the visitor in?" I asked.

"Yeah, but I had no choice."

"You didn't?" I asked. "Were you threatened?"

"Not exactly," he answered.

"Then why did you let him in?" I asked.

"Not him," he said. "She—and there was no way I could keep her out, believe me. Not when she gets like that."

"She?"

He nodded.

I had only met one woman since arriving in town, but what would she be doing up in my room?

"Okay, friend, thanks."

"You're not going to move out, are you?" he asked anxiously.

"Well," I said, "suppose we just see what happens tonight, shall we?"

He shrugged and nodded, and I started upstairs.

Whoever she was she had locked my door behind her, and I used my key to get in.

Sure enough, it was the red-haired girl from the little saloon where I had eaten, and she was sitting on my bed. When she saw me she stood up and placed her hands on her hips.

"Where the hell have you been?" she demanded.

"I'm sorry," I said, "but I didn't know I was going to have company tonight."

She frowned and said, "You make advances at a girl, and then you don't expect her to come to your room?"

"Did I make advances?" I asked.

"You certainly did," she said. "I been around long enough to know when a man is interested, and, mister, you were interested."

"Well, maybe I was," I said, "but right now I'm a little tired."

"Too tired?" she asked.

"Tired," I said.

"Look, let me be honest," she said.

"Please."

"I knew you were interested, and you're not a bad looking fella," she said.

"Thank you."

"I also need someone to take that job I offered you, and I thought maybe I could convince you to take it."

"How did you plan to do that?" I asked.

She sighed and shook her head at me, as if she couldn't understand me.

"How do you think?" she asked.

Her hands went to the buttons of her shirt and she quickly undid them and pulled the shirt off. She wore nothing underneath, and her firm, well-rounded breasts were revealed to me in all their glory. The nipples immediately stood at attention, due more to the cold, I thought, than to any sexual arousal.

"Well," she said, "come on, before I freeze to death."

"You're offering me your body in return for the job?" I asked.

"I'm offering you my body, and we'll discuss the job later," she said.

Well, I thought, standing there with heat welling up in my groin, I was looking for a warm body to share a bed with. Why not?

I walked up to her and took her breasts in my hands. She closed her eyes as I rubbed my palms over her nipples, and then leaned over and licked them.

"Jesus," she said, opening her eyes and looked at her wet, distended nipples, "that's cold. Could we get in bed?"

"Sure," I said.

We both shucked our clothes and hopped into the bed, where the cold sheets were a shock to our naked bodies. We pressed together for warmth, and her flesh was incredibly hot. Her hands immediately went to the swollen column of flesh between my legs, and I reached between her legs and returned the favor. We petted and kissed for a while when she breathed in my ear, "Put it in me, quick. Put it in!"

I climbed on her, careful to keep the blanket on

both of us, and plunged my rigid penis inside of her incredibly hot, wet cavity. The heat that enveloped me was more than welcome; it rapidly traveled the length of my entire body and I could tell that I was stoking a pretty good fire inside of her, too.

She was moaning and clawing at my back, thrusting her hips up to meet mine. I thought I sensed urgency and need in her movements, but she was curiously devoid of passion. She made all of the right moves and sounds, but the desire to give and take pleasure wasn't there. The *need* was, but not the desire.

Pretty soon I felt her go tense underneath, and I let myself go, allowed my seed to surge into her. She wiggled her bottom as I filled her up, and a curious smile came over her face, as if she were relieved to have gotten it over with.

"That was pretty good," she said as I rolled off her.

"Was it?" I said. "You could have fooled me. I'd've sworn you didn't feel a thing," I said, sourly.

"Oh, don't worry, mister," she said, running her hand over my chest, "you were great. I haven't had a man for quite a while, and you sure filled the bill."

"Thanks."

She frowned and propped herself up on one elbow, examining my face.

"Are you angry because I'm not one of those clinging, squealing females who screams when her time comes?"

"I would just have liked a little more . . . participation," I said. "Up here," and I pointed to her head. "I felt like you were miles away, some-where, waiting for it to all be over so you could come back."

"Are you telling me you didn't like it?" she asked, thrusting her furry patch against my thigh, to remind me of how warm it was.

"Oh, I liked it, all right," I said. "Don't wor-ry, you were just great."

She didn't like having her own line thrown back at her, and she showed it. She sat up straight and held the blanket up to her ample chest.

"What about that job?" she asked.

"Not interested," I said.

She turned her head and asked, "Don't you even want to know what it is?"

"I already said I wasn't interested, didn't I?" I asked. "That means there's no need for me to know, right?"

"Will you stop throwing my own lines back in my face!" she said.

"Sorry," I said. "I'm just a little tired, and I don't like trying to be bought with a little pussy."

"A little—" she said, the rest of the words dying in her throat. "You took me to bed knowing you weren't going to take the job?"

"Uh-uh," I said. "You've got it backwards, sweetheart. It was you who took me to bed, remember?"

She tried to get out of bed quickly and got tan-gled up in the blanket. I put my hands behind my head and watched her breasts jiggle and bob as she fought to get free, and then began to get dressed.

"Mister, you're going to be sorry you took ad-vantage of me," she said, while she was dressing.

"What's your name?" I asked her.

"Why?"

"Do you know mine?"

"Sure. I got it off the register downstairs. Clint Adams.

"Well, then, I think it's only fair that I know yours," I said.

"Abby," she said. "Abby O'Shea."

"Okay, Abby, thanks for a very interesting fifteen minutes," I said. "If you ever want to try again, with your heart and your head in it as well as your body, just let me know. I might be in town a while."

She smoldered and stared at me with those pale eyes.

"Mister, if you ever try to stick it in me again, I'll cut the goddamn thing off!"

Without giving me a chance to answer she stormed out of the room and shut the door.

I turned all my attention to trying to get to sleep before the warmth of her body faded from the sheets.

FIVE

The cold woke me up the next morning, so I quickly got dressed and went out looking for something warm to put inside of me.

I decided against going to Abby's little place until I could find out exactly what her story was, so I went back to the saloon where I had played cards the night before.

"What can I get you?" the bartender asked.

"You serving liquor yet?" I asked him.

"Little early," he said, "but I can put some in your coffee if you want."

"Fine. What about food?"

"We serve breakfast," he said, nodding. "Eggs and bacon."

"Great. I'll start now with the coffee."

He poured me a cup of coffee, then threw in a shot of whiskey. I took the cup to a corner table and warmed my hands with it while I waited for breakfast to be ready.

There were a few other early risers having breakfast there, and at one table there was even a small-change poker game going on.

I was watching the front doors when Beauchamp walked in. He spotted me right off and

32

walked on over to my table.

" 'Morning, Clint," he said. "Mind if I sit?"

"Help yourself," I said.

He sat and called over to the bartender that he'd have breakfast.

"Coming up," the bartender told him.

He turned to me then and said, "My first name's André, but my friends call me Andy. We didn't get to that, last night."

"No, but we got to a lot of other stuff," I pointed out. "How much of that Mountie stuff was true?"

He looked at me in surprise and said, "All of it. Don't tell me you didn't believe us?"

"I just wondered why a bunch of deserters would go around talking about it, if it were true."

"Why not?" he asked. "They can't do anything to us here. Canada is another country, you know."

"I suppose you're right, then," I agreed. "How many of you did you say there were?"

"Eighteen, by last count. We're all working up in the mines now, but we're not finding that much to our liking, either."

"At least you're getting paid," I said.

"Small consolation," he assured me. "As fast as we get paid, we lose it in a poker game with some sharpie, like that fella last night. But what else is there to do here?"

"Why do you stay, then?" I asked.

He was about to answer when the bartender came over carrying two plates of eggs and bacon.

Beauchamp rubbed his hands together and said, "And coffee?"

"Only got two hands," the bartender said, good-naturedly. "I'll get it.

"Why do I stay?" Beauchamp went on. He leaned forward and said, "I don't know about the others, but I'm kind of hoping that something will come up, you know?"

"Like what?"

"Oh, like the commissioner sending us a message that he's worked it out so that we can come back, get paid, and not have to face any charges."

"I take it you like being a Mountie?"

He thought that over for a moment, chewing a mouthful of bacon thoughtfully, then said, "As much as I have liked any other job, I guess. It's a lonely life, but there is honor in wearing the uniform, if you know what I mean."

"I suppose I do," I said. There was honor involved during all those years I wore a badge, as well, so I suppose I did understand what he was getting at.

"What do you do?" he asked.

"I just travel," I said. "I fix guns, sometimes I sell them."

"That is a life I have not tried," he admitted. "Traveling. I was born in Canada and this is the first time I have been outside of my own country."

"Are you French?" I asked, detecting a slight accent.

"Yes, but I have been speaking more English than French for most of my life," he said. Judging from the way he looked, that might have been about thirty years.

"So what made you desert?" I asked.

"Oh, I don't know," he said. "I was discontented over not having been paid, but that was not it. Perhaps it was the pressure from the others, my friends who wanted to do it, but would not unless I came along. I could not ruin it for them," he said.

"And then there was the adventure involved," I added. "Wasn't that it, too?"

He smiled sheepishly and said, "Yes, I admit it. It was an opportunity to leave my country for the first time in my life, but now . . ." He let it trail off as a serious expression came over his face and he began to toy with his food.

"What is it?" I asked.

He looked at me and said, "I believe that for the first time it has struck me that I may not be able to go back to my country ever again."

"So you'll stay here and wait, hoping to hear word that you will be welcomed back," I said, and he nodded. "Well, I can't say I blame you for that, Andy. I do have some advice for you, though."

"What is it?"

"Try to stay out of poker games with people you don't know, and save your money."

"Ha!" he laughed, shaking his head. "Even if we do not spend our money on poker, there is Miss Lottie's."

"I've heard about her place," I said.

"Ah, the women there are the finest for hundreds of miles," he said, looking dreamy eyed. "I will take you there tonight, my friend."

"I don't think so, Andy," I said.

"And why not?" he asked.

"I'm not in the habit of paying for my pleasure," I said.

"Ah, but that is the wonderful part," he said.

"You can play poker there as well as here," he explained, "but there, if you win, you do not win money."

"I think I see what you're getting at," I said. "That might be interesting, at that."

"Good, then you will come. I must go to work now," he said, pushing away his empty plate, "but I will meet you here later this evening, say six o'clock?"

"Fine," I said. "I'll be here."

"See you then, my friend," he said. He stood up and began to reach into his pocket to pay for his breakfast.

"The breakfast is my pleasure," I said to him. "I insist."

"If you insist, I will not argue," he said, smiling broadly. "I will see you this evening."

SIX

Usually when I arrive in a town I let the sheriff know, because I have a reputation that sometimes attracts trouble. In this case, however, since I wasn't sure whether my "fame" had spread to the Northwest or not, I decided to tell the local law that I was checking in with him, give him my name, and not supply any further information unless he recognized it.

As I was paying the bartender for breakfast, I asked him where the sheriff's office was.

"That's on Silver Street," he said. "Go out here, make a right and walk to Main Street, then turn left and walk a block until you come to Silver Street. You'll see it."

"Okay, thanks. The breakfast was real good."

"Thanks. I'll tell my missus. She does the cooking."

"What happens when breakfast is over and the drinkers start coming in?" I asked.

"She goes home until lunch time, and then she goes home until dinner time. Serving food makes us a lot of extra money, but I don't like her to hang around here unless she's cooking. Sometimes there's trouble."

"I know what you mean," I said. "Listen, have you lived in this town long?"

"All my life," he said, "and I got no urge to go anywhere else."

He was a big, bearish looking man with heavy, sloping shoulders and large, hairy hands. I was sure that whenever trouble did arise in his place, he pretty much took care of it on his own.

"What can you tell me about Abby O'Shea?" I said. "We've crossed paths once or twice since I got here yesterday."

"She's a cold one, Abby is," he said. "Pretty, but cold inside. She came here about a year ago and set up shop in that little place of hers, selling a little of everything."

"She doesn't do much business, does she?"

"You wouldn't think so," he said, "but she don't seem to be suffering none."

"So where does she get her money?"

"I couldn't tell you that, mister, because I don't know. If she'd run a table in there—and one would be all she could fit—she'd do a lot more business, but it don't seem to bother her that her place is almost always empty."

"Does she get along with the people in town?" I asked.

"She don't have no friends, but then she don't have no enemies, either. She pretty much keeps to herself."

"I see."

"If you got any interest in Abby," he said, "you'd be better off going on over to Miss Lottie's. The women over there are a lot warmer and friendlier."

"Now how would you know that," I asked,

"what with you being a married man, and all?"

He grinned at me and picked up a wet rag in his huge hand and began wiping the bartop with it.

"I hear things," he replied, still grinning.

"Yeah," I said, "I'll bet you do. Thanks for the directions, and the advice."

"You come back tonight, friend," he said, "and the second round of drinks will be on the house."

"You got a deal," I told him, and left to go and find the sheriff's office on Silver Street.

SEVEN

The sheriff's office was a small, new, brick and adobe building. Above the door there was a sign that said Sheriff's Office. Alongside the door was another sign: John Tambor, Sheriff.

I knocked on the heavy oak door and received an invitation to enter. I assumed that the man standing behind the desk was Sheriff Tambor, and the star on his chest confirmed it.

"What can I do for you, stranger?" he asked.

Tambor was a slim man of about forty who wore a tired down Remington on his left hip. He was well dressed, with a pastel shirt and a string tie. I knew that when he came out from behind his desk his boots would be spit polished. There was another pair of boots in a corner, cracked and well-worn, and I had an idea that if he had to leave his office, he changed boots.

Tambor was a dandy, and probably fancied himself a ladies' man. I disliked him on the spot, and he'd only spoken seven words to me.

"I just got into town yesterday, Sheriff," I explained, "and thought I'd check in with the local law."

"You wanted?"

"No."

"On the run from anybody?"

"No."

"Why you checking in, then?" he asked, frowning.

"I used to be a lawman," I said. "I know how important it is to keep track of strangers in town. I just thought I'd make your job a little easier, that's all."

"What's your name?" he asked, sitting back down behind his desk.

I stayed where I was, just inside the door, and said, "Clint Adams."

"Where are you staying?"

"In a hotel," I said. "Don't know the name, but the 'o' is missing on the sign—"

"Deke Manson's place," he said. "You must be his only guest."

"Guess that means I'll get good service," I commented, and he smiled, as if he knew something I didn't.

"Okay, friend, you checked in. Just watch your step and we won't have any reason to meet again. How long you figure on staying?"

"Haven't decided yet."

"Let me know when you do," he said. He looked down at his shirt and brushed off a spec that only he could see. When he looked up, he seemed surprised that I was still there. "That's all," he said.

When I left, he was brushing a few more invisible specs from the sleeves of his pretty shirt. I had noticed that the gun on his hip could have used some maintenance.

I never had any respect for a man who took better care of his clothes than of his gun.

EIGHT

Outside the cold began to cut into my skin again, and I decided that maybe I needed some kind of a jacket.

Who better to buy it from than Abby O'Shea?

That young lady seemed to fascinate me more and more, and I was wondering what sort of job it was she needed a man for. Curiosity about her and the job, plus the need for a jacket, gave me enough excuses to go and see her again.

What the bartender had told me about her being a cold woman had been something I'd discovered myself the night before. I couldn't help wondering what she'd be like in bed if she put her mind to it.

When I walked into her place it was empty, as I had expected, only I hadn't expected her to be missing as well. I could have walked out of there with anything I wanted, if I'd had a mind to.

"Hello?" I called out.

No answer.

"Abby O'Shea!" I called. "Anybody here?"

A curtain behind the counter moved and her head appeared. She looked puzzled, and then when she saw me she looked . . . disappointed.

"Oh, it's you," she said.

"Who were you expecting?" I asked.

"Nobody," she said, coming out from behind the curtain. She was wearing a man's shirt and a pair of jeans, and made them look good.

"You know, you could lose a lot of stock leaving the place untended," I pointed out, walking up to the counter. "Is that why you need someone?"

"Who says I need someone?" she asked, belligerently.

"You said you needed someone for a job," I reminded her.

"Oh, that," she said. "No, that's got nothing to do with this place."

"What then?"

She ignored the question and said, "What do you want here?"

"A jacket," I said. "Something warm."

"Fur lined," she said. She reached under the counter and came up with one, denim with a fur lining.

"I'll take it," I said. She told me how much it was and I paid her, then slid the thing right on.

"Is that all?"

"What makes you so mean?" I asked.

"Maybe it's men who take advantage of me," she replied.

"Now wait a minute," I said. "You came to my room last night, remember? I didn't invite you."

"Forget it," she said. "I got work to do."

"Sure," I said. "I just figured maybe we could start over again, become friends."

"I doubt it," she said. "I don't have time for friends."

"I'm sorry to hear that," I said.

"I got work," she said again. "Is there anything else?"

"No, Abby," I said. "Nothing else. You go ahead and finish with your work. I hope you get great satisfaction from it."

"I intend to," she said, and disappeared behind the curtain, once again leaving her stock alone, for the taking.

NINE

I spent most of the day exploring the town. To my delight I found a place that advertised hot baths in warm rooms. The proprietor assured me that I would be able to dry off after my bath without freezing my behind off. Remembering that Andy Beauchamp had promised to take me to Miss Lottie's, I decided to take a chance.

Lazing in the hot water was wonderful, and the temperature in the room was considerably warmer than it was outside. I don't know exactly how they did it, but whatever it was, when I got out of the tub I was able to take my time drying off, and never even felt a chill.

I felt considerably refreshed and comfortable when I left the bathhouse, a condition that lasted about two blocks once I got back out into the cold. By now it was nearly time to meet Beauchamp, so I stopped at my hotel for a change of clothing, and headed for the saloon feeling clean, refreshed, and cold. I arrived before Andy.

"I need some warming up," I told the bartender.

"This stuff will do it," he assured me, pouring

me a glass. "Not used to the cold weather, huh?"

"Not this cold," I said. "I've run across some cold winters in Oklahoma, and Texas, but this . . ." I said, trailing off and drinking the whiskey down. It burned its way to my stomach, where it nestled, starting a small fire.

"Montana cold is almost as bad as Canada," he said.

"That I wouldn't know," I said. "I've never been that far north. Hell, I'd never been this far north until now. How about another shot?"

"Sure," he said, pouring out another.

I drank half of that one, then looked around the place. The dealers were busy taking the customers' money from them.

"I don't think we've exchanged names, friend," the bartender said. He extended one huge hand. "Mine's Flynn, Jake Flynn."

"Adams," I said. "Clint Adams." I put my hand in his and hoped he wouldn't crush it. He controlled the strength in his hand and gave me back mine still in one piece.

"Seen the town yet?" he asked. I told him I'd had a look around. "It's a little bigger than most mining towns," he went on. "It might even be bigger, if we was getting a little more gold out of those mines, but they're about played out."

"What happens when it's all gone?" I asked.

He shrugged. "A lot of people will move on, and we'll settle down into being a nice, small, poor town."

"What will you do?"

"Stick around," he answered without hesitation. "After all, it is my home."

I nodded and finished off my drink. "Tell me

about Lottie's," I said. "Beauchamp—one of the miners—"

"I know Andy," Flynn said.

"Yeah, well, I told Andy I don't pay for my women, but he told me I didn't have to at Miss Lottie's."

"That's not exactly true. Lottie lets you gamble for her girls. If you lose, you lose money; if you win, you win an hour—or a night—with one of the girls in the pot."

"One of the girls in the pot?"

" *You* bet money," he explained, "and her *dealers* bet girls. The more money you have in the pot, the longer you get one of her girls for . . . if you win."

"Sounds clever."

"It works," he said, "seeing as how the house always has the odds in their favor."

That was for sure. No gambling house would be able to make money if it weren't.

I was still standing at the bar with my eye on the mirror, when Andy Beauchamp walked in.

He clapped me on the shoulder from behind and said, "Are you ready for an interesting evening, my friend?"

"I am if you are," I said.

"I will be, after a drink," he replied.

"Where are your friends?" I asked him as he accepted a beer from Jake Flynn.

"They will be at Lottie's," he assured me.

"What's this Miss Lottie herself like?" I asked.

The eyes of both Jake Flynn and Andy Beauchamp lit up as Andy said, "Ah, Miss Lottie, yes. Out of all the lovely girls she has in her establishment, none can match her beauty and grace."

"Is that so?" I said, getting more interested by the moment.

"She does not dally with the customers, however," Andy said. "She simply supplies the girls."

"If she's as beautiful as you say she is," I said, "that sounds like a damned waste."

"It is, my friend, it is," Beauchamp said.

TEN

On our way to Lottie's Andy said, "Jake's wife should know that he has been to the Pleasure Palace once or twice."

"Or more?" I added.

Andy laughed and said, "Whenever he gets the chance. Have you seen Mrs. Flynn?"

"Not yet."

"A wonderful woman," he said, "and a marvelous cook, but when it comes to beauty and grace, I would take your horse."

"Have you seen my horse?" I asked.

"It does not matter," he assured me, and we both laughed. "He does love her, though," he added.

Miss Lottie's was across the street from my hotel, which meant that it was not exactly in the heart of town, or in the best district. Still, the place was the biggest and most eyecatching building in that area. "Miss Lottie's Pleasure Palace" was painted in tall, bright yellow letters, and the dingy buildings on either side were made that much dingier.

"Very impressive," I said as we approached the front door. There was music and laughter coming from within, and the evening sounded as if it were in full swing.

"You are going to enjoy this, Clint," Andy Beauchamp said. "If you enjoy women and gambling, this is the place for you."

We entered, and I found myself in a single, gigantic room that was so well lit it looked like daylight inside. There were tables set up all around with dealers and customers squaring off. Behind each dealer stood two or three girls, all of whom appeared to be very pretty and healthy, wearing low-cut, glittering gowns.

"How many girls does she have?" I asked.

"No one knows for sure," Andy said. "She might have as many as forty or fifty."

That was a lot of girls for a single whorehouse to have, and I said so.

"Oh, this is much more than just another whorehouse, Clint. Do you want to play?"

"I think I'll watch for a while," I said, "but you go ahead."

He led me to a poker table where the dealer was telling an irate player, "Five hands is the maximum, friend. If you don't take a hand, you can move on to another table."

The customer had his eye on a girl standing behind the dealer, though, and didn't want to move on to another table.

"I want a shot at that dark-eyed gal," the man insisted.

"Then you can get up and wait your turn again," the dealer said. "But there are other tables open, and all of the girls are of the same quality."

"They ain't got that gal's dark eyes," the customer insisted. He looked like a miner, still dressed in the dirty clothes he had worked that day in. Apparently, he couldn't wait to clean up and change when his shift was done and had rushed right over straight from work.

I looked at the dark-eyed girl he was talking about, and found that she was not especially pretty and did not have that good a body, but she did have these two enormous, dark eyes, and I could almost understand the miner's interest.

"Look, friend," the dealer said, "don't make me call for help—"

"That won't be necessary," Andy Beauchamp said, stepping in. "Come on, Dan," he said, taking hold of the miner beneath the right elbow, "let someone else have a chance."

The miner called Dan looked up at Beauchamp, who had a tight, insistent grip on the other man's arm and was trying to send him a message with his eyes.

"We don't want any trouble, do we?" Beauchamp asked.

"No," Dan agreed reluctantly. "No trouble."

He stood up, still watching the dark-eyed girl who was smiling suggestively at him, and I knew he'd be back in that chair as soon as he possibly could.

"That was close," Andy said. "Lottie may have the most beautiful girls, but she also has the biggest bouncers."

"I guess you saved him a headache," I said, referring to the big miner called Dan.

"Oh, no," Andy said, looking at me in surprise.

"I saved Lottie the trouble of hiring new bouncers. Dan Dupree can break any three men I know into six pieces."

ELEVEN

Andy Beauchamp pulled out the chair Dan Dupree had just gotten up from and sat down, pulling out his money.

"How much do you want to play for?" the dealer asked. He turned in his chair with a bored look on his face and said, "Mindy, Diane or Linda."

The dark-eyed girl was the one he called Diane, and Andy Beauchamp pointed to her and said, "Diane."

"Minimum bet, ten dollars," the dealer said.

"Deal," Andy told him.

"Seven card stud," the dealer said, and quickly dealt out two cards down and one up for each of them.

Beauchamp was dealt a king of spades on the table, but a pair of deuces in the hole. The dealer had a ten of hearts showing.

"Ten dollars," Andy said.

I watched the dealer very closely as he worked. He dealt Andy a jack of spades, and gave himself a nine of hearts.

"King bets," he said, and Andy bet another ten dollars. This time, instead of simply calling, the dealer raised ten dollars, and Andy called.

"Next card," the dealer said, and doled them out.

Andy received a three of spades, and the dealer caught another nine, giving him a pair.

"Twenty dollars," the dealer said, and Andy called.

"Next card," the dealer said. He dealt Andy a deuce of spades, giving him four spades on the table, but also three deuces. A strong hand, with a good chance for improvement.

The dealer caught another heart, this one a six, giving him three hearts and a pair of nines on the table.

The dealer was still high with his nines, and he bet twenty dollars. Andy, sitting with three deuces and a potential spade flush, raised twenty dollars. Surprisingly, the dealer reraised him twenty dollars, and Andy called. Whatever the dealer had, it was a heck of a lot more than two nines. He might have had two hearts in the hole for a heart flush, but if Andy made his spade flush, it would be at least king high, and the house dealer would need an ace-high flush to beat it.

"Last card," the dealer said.

While Andy was throwing cash into the pot, the dealer was throwing in colored chips with numbers on them. I assumed that these chips were redeemable for the services of the dark-eyed girl named Diane. The length of service probably depended on how many chips a customer had.

Andy checked his last card, and it was a king of clubs. He had missed his spade flush, but instead had made a full house, deuces over kings.

With nines on the table, the dealer said, "Forty dollars."

Andy wanted to raise, but he didn't have enough cash. I wondered for a moment if he was going to turn to me to ask if he could borrow some, but to his credit he did not.

"I call," Andy said, putting in forty dollars.

"Nines full," the dealer said, turning his cards over. He had three nines, a pair of sixes. The third nine and second six were in the hole.

"Damn," Andy Beauchamp said, turning his cards over. He had lost to a larger full house, which is one of the toughest ways to lose in poker.

I had watched the dealer the whole time, and he had dealt a clean game.

Andy stood up and the dark-eyed girl gave him a look that said, "Go get some more money and come on back."

She turned those eyes on these miners, and they bet their last cent to try and get her upstairs, where I assumed the rooms were.

"Your turn," Andy said to me, shrugging helplessly.

I sat down.

"How much?" the dealer asked, looking bored. "Mindy, Diane—"

"Diane," I said, interrupting him. "Go ahead, deal."

TWELVE

"Seven card stud," the dealer said. They played that because it involved the most cards, the most opportunities to make a bet.

I received the king of diamonds and the ten of spades in the hole, and the queen of clubs on the table. The dealer showed a four of hearts.

"Queen bets," he said. "Ten dollar minimum bet."

I had learned a couple of things while watching Andy play. Number one, you can't bluff, because all they've got at stake is a night with a whore. They could make that back easy on the next guy. Number two, don't raise, because if you win, you win. It's as easy as that. If you raise, you're just trying for an extra half hour or hour with the whore, that's all.

"Ten dollars."

"Call," the dealer said. I couldn't understand why the dealer didn't raise every time, drawing more hard cash into the pot. Then again, I figured, there are certain instincts you develop when you play poker, and raising on nothing is something you don't do.

He dealt out our next card. I got a seven of

clubs to his ten of diamonds.

"Queen bets," he said.

"Ten dollars."

"Call," he said. "Next card."

I looked up at the object of all this effort, and she turned those eyes on me with a look that was supposed to make me forget how to play cards.

I got a two of hearts, and he got an ace of spades, which put him in the lead.

"Ten dollars," he said.

"Call," I said. Then I said, "Next card," beating him to it. He gave me a dirty look; I had upset his sequence.

"Next card," he said anyway, to get himself back on the right track.

He dealt me an ace of clubs, and himself another ace, this one a heart.

"Pair of aces bets forty dollars," he said.

He jumped from ten to forty, probably to get me back for stepping on his line.

I needed a jack for a straight. He had two aces on the table, with a four and a ten. Two aces and two hearts showing. I had one of his aces, and there were no jacks out, so I called.

"Last card," he said, dealing them.

I checked my hole card and when he said, "Forty dollars," I called.

"Two pair," he said. "Aces and fours."

"Straight to the ace," I said, showing my hole cards. My last card had been the jack I needed.

"Why didn't you raise?" he demanded.

"What for?" I asked, pulling my cash back and collecting my chips.

"Because that's the way the game is played." he replied, angrily.

"Only when you're playing for real, friend," I told him, putting my money away.

"Ain't you gonna give us a chance to get even?" he asked, watching my money disappear into my pocket.

I grabbed one of Andy's hands and filled it with the chips I'd won and said, "Take it up with my friend, here."

Andy looked at the chips, then at the dark-eyed girl and said, "Thanks."

"Don't mention it," I said.

I was walking away when he said, "How long does this get me with her?"

I don't think either of us heard the answer because there was a loud roar that drowned it out. I turned quickly and saw Dan Dupree descending on Andy, shouting, "You took my woman!"

"Dan, wait—" Beauchamp shouted, but big Dan wasn't waiting for anything.

I had won the chips and given them to Andy, so if he absorbed a beating, it would be my fault. I took off and when Dupree threw himself at Andy, I threw myself between them.

I grabbed Dupree around the waist and the two of us went flying into the poker table, upsetting it and the dealer, and scattering the girls behind it.

"Mine," Dupree was shouting, trying to get untangled from me and the table.

"Settle down, Dupree," I shouted, but he wouldn't listen.

I regained my balance first and clubbed him with a right hand he barely felt. He swung his left at me in a vicious backhand that I narrowly avoided, and then I hit him with two quick punches, a left and a right. He fell over onto his back, but I got careless and he hit me in the side with his boot, sending me sprawling to the floor.

"Dan!" I heard Andy yell, but Dupree wasn't listening to anyone. He didn't care who he was fighting now, he just wanted to fight.

"Dan, no," Andy said, moving forward, but Dupree hit him with a right that knocked over another poker table. I got quickly to my feet, and when the big man turned to look for me I hit him with my right again, knocking him back a few steps.

"Shit," I said, because my blows were barely slowing him down, and I had no intention of using my gun.

As he came for me again, I picked up a chair and hit him across the chest with it. He staggered back as the chair splintered, leaving me with just a leg in my hand. I stepped in and jabbed the chair leg into his stomach, doubling him up, and then I brought it down on the back of his head. He grunted and fell to his hands and knees, shaking his large head back and forth to try and clear it. He tried to get to his feet, lost his balance and fell over onto his side, still conscious, but stunned.

I had no intention of hitting him again with the chair leg, for fear that I might hurt him badly, but one of the bouncers had no such fear. He came wading in with a big club and prepared to bring it down over the fallen man's head.

"No," I said, moving forward and grabbing his wrist. "Don't hit him."

"Get outta my way," the man growled, pushing me away. "This is my job," he said, with obvious joy in his eyes. This was clearly his favorite part of the job and he didn't want anyone interfering.

The bouncer himself was a good-sized man and I didn't feel like going a round with him, so as he lifted his club again I stepped in and hit him with the chair leg. His head was not as hard as Dupree's, and he keeled over like a felled tree.

"Clint, watch out!" I heard Andy yell. I turned in time to see another bouncer coming at me with a club.

"This is getting out of hand," I said to no one in particular. I avoided the bouncer's lunge and then tapped him on the bridge of his nose with my trusty chair leg. He howled and backed up, trying to stop the flow of blood that was gushing from his nostrils.

I felt someone behind me and turned with the chair leg raised, but it was Andy Beauchamp and he said, "Whoa, easy!" His eye was rapidly swelling from Dan Dupree's punch.

"I think we ought to leave," I said, "before they call in reinforcements."

"We have to take Dan," he said, pointing to Dupree, who was still struggling to regain his feet.

"What?"

"He's my friend," he insisted.

"Some friend," I said, but I dropped the chair leg and we bent over and each took one of his arms. "Let's go," I said, and we half walked, half dragged him towards the front door. As we approached it, though, we spotted three men standing in front of it, all holding clubs.

"Oh, shit," I said. I didn't want to pull out my gun, because I rarely do unless I intend to use it, but neither was I going to allow myself to be beaten to a pulp by three men with large clubs.

Luckily, the door behind them opened and in

stepped Sheriff John Tambor.

"All right," he shouted. "What's going on?"

The dealer I'd been playing cards with stepped forward and, pointing at us, said, "Those three started a brawl, Sheriff."

Tambor looked at us, then looked at the two bouncers I'd hit.

"All right, Adams," he said. "You and your two friends can just keep walking until you get to my jailhouse. We'll settle this in the morning, after you've all had a good night's sleep."

"Our pleasure, Sheriff," I assured him. "Come on," I told Andy. On the way out we both smiled at the three bouncers with the clubs. When we reached the sheriff I was about to thank him when Dan Dupree got us into even more trouble than we were already in.

He belched, and then threw up on Sheriff Tambor's boots.

THIRTEEN

I had been in jail before, spent the night in a cell before, but the door had always been open, and I had always been free to walk in and out as I pleased. That was because I used to run the place.

This, however, was something new to me. The door was locked and I didn't have the keys.

"This is the first time you've even been in jail?" Andy asked, looking surprised.

"I've always been on the other side of the locked door, Andy," I told him.

"Well, then, you know he won't keep us in here for very long," he said.

"No," I agreed. "We'll be let out today and given a fine, but that doesn't make it feel any better."

We had our own cells, right next to one another. Dan Dupree had been taken out for medical attention the night before, and had never been brought back. I was hoping that I hadn't hit him too hard.

"Don't worry," Andy told me when I voiced my worry. "Dan has a hard head."

"I'm sorry I hit him," I said. "I know he's your friend, but I thought he was going to kill you, and I was the one who had given you those chips."

"Don't worry about it," he said. "Dan won't hold a grudge. He gets like that sometimes, that's all. He's a good man to have on your side in a fight."

"I can believe that," I said, looking at his face. "How does that eye feel?"

"Sore," he said, touching it gingerly. It had not quite closed on him, but there was little more than a slit for him to see through. "It's okay," he assured me. He laughed and said, "Guess our big night didn't turn out the way we planned, huh?"

"Sorry," I said, "but that kind of poker isn't as interesting to me as the real thing. The dealer's got nothing to lose."

"I can see that," he said. "But still, I lost all of my money last night. That girl with the dark eyes . . ." he said, shaking his head.

She was skinny, although she did have a rather large set of breasts. Still, there was something about those eyes, all right . . .

We heard a key turn and then the sheriff entered the cell block. He had rushed out of his office the night before without changing out of his spit-polished boots and he had turned livid when Dupree puked on them. I looked at them now, and they were black and shiny again.

"Got your boots clean, I see," I said, because I still didn't like him.

"Don't push me, Adams," he said. "I'm letting you and your friends off with a fine, but if I charged you for a new pair of boots it would cost you even more than that."

He opened the door to Andy's cell first, and

then mine. Before walking out of the cell I took a last look around and thought to myself, *So that's how it feels.*

I walked through the door and out to freedom, hoping I'd never again have to spend a night like the one I'd just spent.

Out in his office the sheriff gave us back our personal belongings, but tried to keep the Colt New Line I usually kept tucked into my belt, inside my shirt.

"The other gun, Sheriff," I said, holding out my hand for it.

He glared at me, but opened his top drawer, took it out and handed it to me.

"Guess I forgot," he said.

"Like hell," I said, and then turned to Andy and said, "Let's get the hell out of here. I'll buy you breakfast."

"Fine with me."

"Adams," Tambor said, standing up.

"Yeah?" I asked over my shoulder with my hand on the door knob.

"Stay out of trouble," he said. "I'm letting you off easy this time because you used to be a lawman, but next time, no favors. Got it?"

"I've got it, Sheriff," I said.

Outside, Andy said, "I've got just enough time for breakfast before going to work."

"After we eat, I'll check on Dan Dupree's condition," I said.

"Don't bother," he said. "I'm sure I'll see him at work. I'll tell him you were worried. He'll appreciate it."

"Is he a Mountie, too?" I asked.

"He is," Andy said as we headed for the saloon

for breakfast. "He's the one who really convinced me that I should come with them," he added.

"What was his argument?" I asked.

Andy laughed and said, "He said he needed someone to keep him out of trouble."

FOURTEEN

After breakfast Andy went to work and I worked on another pot of coffee laced liberally with whiskey. I was trying to wash away the bad dreams I'd had while trying to sleep inside that cell.

I had dreamed that I was in prison, sharing a cell with everyone I had ever arrested and sent to prison. None of them did anything to me. They all just sat there, staring at me, and in my dream I had been afraid to go to sleep, for I knew that was when they would all jump me.

I shivered and poured out the last cup of coffee from the pot.

"Heard you had quite a time last night," Jake said, joining me.

"It was one I could have done without," I assured him.

"The way I heard it, you laid out about a dozen of Lottie's bouncers before the sheriff came to cart you away."

"A dozen?" I asked, smiling. "The way stories get built up."

"It wasn't a dozen?" he asked, looking disappointed.

"No," I said. "It was only eleven."

I didn't want him to stay disappointed.

"Man," he said, flexing his fingers, "I wish I had been there. I haven't had a good fight in a long time."

"Next time I'll call you," I promised.

"I'll hold you to that," he said, and then got up to take care of a customer.

When he finished with the customer he came back to the table as I was ready to leave and said, "Oh, yeah, I almost forgot."

"What?"

"Lottie wants to meet you."

I stared at him and then said, "Lottie, from Miss Lottie's?"

"That's the one."

"Why does she want to meet me?"

"Guess she must have missed the fun, last night. Maybe she wants to hire you to replace those eleven bouncers."

"Maybe," I said. "Does she live in her place?"

"Nah, Lottie's got herself a house, down at the south end of town. Can't miss it. It's the biggest one down there."

"That's not the best part of town, is it?" I said.

"If it was, Lottie wouldn't be living there."

"Okay, Jake, thanks. I'll pay her a visit."

"You better clean up, first," he said. "You ain't gonna make any kind of impression looking and smelling the way you do."

"You're right," I said. "I'll grab some clean clothes and head over to the bathhouse."

"Get yourself a nice shave, too," he said, raising his eyebrows and making eyes at me. "Lottie likes her men clean."

"Now how would you know that?" I asked him.

He grinned broadly and said, "I hear things."

FIFTEEN

After I left the bathhouse—leaving behind the clothing I was wearing to be cleaned, except for the jacket—I took Jake's advice and went and got a shave. Feeling human and clean again, I started walking towards the south end of town. I remembered then that I had wanted to check on Dan Dupree, but that would mean going back to Sheriff Tambor to find out where he had been taken, and I wasn't up to talking with the sheriff again. I'd just have to wait to hear from Andy Beauchamp, and hope that Dupree had indeed been at work, as Andy had predicted.

When I reached the end of town I saw why Jake had told me I couldn't miss Miss Lottie's house. There was a picket fence surrounding it, and it was painted the same yellow as the Pleasure Palace was. I walked to the gate and found it open, walked to the front door and knocked. After a few moments, the door was answered by a small, young black maid.

"Yes?" she asked.

"I'd like to see Miss Lottie," I said.

"Miss Lottie don't see no one outside of the Palace," she said, making it sound as if we were talking about a royal palace, and not the Pleasure Palace.

"I think she'll see me," I said.

"I doubts it," she said. "What's yore name?"

"Clint Adams," I said.

"You wait there, I'll tell her," the girl said, and shut the door in my face. I waited on the front steps and eventually the girl returned, looking at me with renewed respect.

"Miss Lottie say she'll see you, suh," she said.

"Well, I knew that," I said, stepping into the house.

She closed the door and said, "This way, suh."

I followed her down a long hall, impressed by the size of Miss Lottie's home. It must have been the profits from the "Palace" that had enabled her to get it, which didn't surprise me. I hadn't particularly liked the operation from a customer's standpoint, but from a business standpoint it was a fabulous idea.

"Miss Lottie want you to join her for coffee in the dining room," the maid said.

I followed her through a set of French doors into the dining room. The maid left then, leaving me alone with the woman seated at the table who was, to say the least, impressive. To say the most, she was possibly the best damned looking woman I had ever seen.

Her age was somewhere between thirty and forty, but that didn't matter at all. She had dark hair swept up on her head, and a long, graceful neck. Her eyes were the shape of a cat's, and I wasn't sure of their color. I suspected that the color would change with what she wore. At the moment she was wearing a powder blue robe that appeared to be made from silk, tied at her waist and pushed out by full, well-rounded breasts.

"Mr. Adams?" she asked.

"Yes, ma'am," I said.

She didn't rise from the table, but invited me over to sit.

"Please," she said, "join me. Lulu will bring us coffee shortly. Something to eat?"

"I had breakfast, thank you," I said. "Just coffee will be fine."

"Very well," she said. "I understand you spent the night in jail."

"That's right," I said. "Things seemed to get out of hand at your place last night. I'm sorry if there was any damage. I'd be glad to pay—"

"Nonsense," she said, waving away my offer. "It's all been taken care of."

Lulu came in with a fresh pot of coffee and a cup and saucer for me. She poured me some, and then left us alone.

"Excuse me, Miss Lottie—" I began, but she cut me off.

"Don't call me that," she said. "That's just what's painted on the wall outside the palace. My name is Leticia Newman. You can call me Miss Newman or, if you're comfortable with it, Leticia."

"That's a lovely name," I said. "But then why shouldn't it be, considering the woman who bears it."

She looked at me with wide eyes and said, "My God, a man who knows how to use words as well as his fists."

"Actually," I said, picking up my coffee, "I used a chair leg to do most of the damage."

"And honest, too," she said. "My, what a rare find you are, Mr. Adams."

"Not so rare, ma'am," I said.

"Leticia," she said.

"Leticia."

"Are you modest, as well?" she asked.

"I don't think so," I said. "I know what I'm good at, but I don't make a habit of passing it around."

"What are you good at, Mr. Adams?"

I shrugged, wondering what this was all leading up to.

"Poker, guns—"

"Fixing them, or using them?" she asked.

"Both."

"What else?"

I shrugged again, and she said, "Women?"

I hesitated, then said, "I've had my moments."

"Yes," she said, studying me critically. "I can believe that you have."

"Leticia," I said, "forgive me for being so blunt—"

"You'd like to know why I wanted to see you," she finished for me.

"Yes."

"Curiosity, I suppose," she said. "Benjamin—that was the dealer you played against last night—was very upset after playing you. No one has ever upset Benjamin, before."

"That's rough," I said, without sympathy.

"Also, no one has ever beaten up two of my bouncers before," she said.

"I told you, I used a chair leg."

"And they were armed with clubs," she pointed

out. "Why didn't you use your gun?"

"There was no need," I said.

"They might have beaten you to death."

"Perhaps," I said, "but they didn't."

"No," she said, thoughtfully, "they didn't. Mr. Adams, you wouldn't by any chance be interested in a job, would you?"

Why did all of the women I met in Helena want to hire me? I kept my curiosity from getting the best of me and said, "No, I wouldn't."

"You haven't asked what kind."

"It wouldn't matter," I told her. "Thank you for the coffee."

"I haven't finished talking to you," she said.

"But I've finished talking to you," I said.

"Are you going to be rude now?" she asked, looking amused.

"Of course not," I said, standing. "I'll say excuse me, and be on my way."

"You are a rare man, Mr. Adams, in spite of what you say," she told me.

"I won't argue with a lady," I said.

"I would like to be able to talk to you again, another time," she said.

"Fine," I said. "Next time we'll have breakfast at my hotel. Good day, Leticia. I can find my way out."

"Good day, Mr. Adams," she said from behind me. "We'll talk again."

Sure, I thought, only next time I hope one of us *says* something.

SIXTEEN

As cold as it was out, it felt so good to be out of jail that I strolled a bit around the town. There was the city hall, right across the street from the bathhouse, and the Bank of Helena, right behind Abby's little saloon, and adjacent to Miss Lottie's Pleasure Palace. I guess that made it easy for Lottie to get there with her day's receipts, and maybe that was where Abby had her big nest egg socked away, which was why she didn't care about her lack of customers. I also located the Church of Helena, which I didn't go into, and I found a saloon called North Texas, which I did go into.

I bought a beer and asked the bartender how the place came to be called North Texas.

"I'm from Texas," he said, "and I own the place. What else would I call it? Are you from Texas?"

I shook my head.

"I came from the East originally, then Oklahoma, but lately I've been spending most of my time in the Southwest, and a lot of it in Texas. That's why I was curious."

"Well, you're welcome in here anytime," he

said. "There's usually a few Texans in here, having a hell of a time."

"I'll remember," I said, putting down my empty beer mug. "Thanks for the hospitality."

"Texas hospitality is the best kind," he said, and I left.

After Texas North, I went back to Jake Flynn's place, which he simply called Flynn's.

"How did it go?" he asked with great anticipation.

"She offered me a job," I said.

"Doing what?"

"I didn't ask."

"You turned her down?"

"Yeah. Give me a beer, will you?"

He went and got the beer and put it down in front of me, asking, "Why'd you turn her down?"

"Since I got here, Jake, I've met two women, and they've both offered me jobs."

"What was the other one?"

"That was from Abby O'Shea, and I didn't ask her what it was, either," I said.

"I guess you ain't looking for a job," he said.

"No," I said, "I'm not, but I'm suspicious about women who offer jobs to men they don't know."

"Maybe you're just suspicious of women," he proposed.

"Or maybe I'm just plain suspicious," I said. "Do you know a miner named Dan Dupree?"

"Sure, I know Dan," he said. "He was involved in that brawl last night, wasn't he?"

"Yeah, only I didn't realize that he and Andy Beauchamp were friends. I thought he was going to kill Andy, which was why I stepped in."

"Well, he might have," Jake said. "When Dan has a few, sometimes he doesn't know what he's doing. He's a hell of a nice guy, but he can't hold his liquor."

"I guess he really does need someone to keep him out of trouble," I said, only half aloud.

"That's more than a one man job," Jake said.

"Did you hear anything about his condition today?" I asked.

"No, but I wouldn't worry," he said. "I've seen Dan take some pretty hard blows."

"Jake, are these fellas—Andy Beauchamp, Dan Dupree, some of the others—are they really deserters from the Canadian Mounties?"

"That's what they say," he answered. "They were wearing civilian clothing when they arrived, but I believe what they say about having gone over the border."

"Yeah, I guess I do, too, but I wanted to see if anyone else did," I said. "I hope for their sake that things work out okay."

"They're a good bunch of guys," Jake said. "Most of them drink and play cards in here, and they're pretty well behaved."

"Except for Dupree," I pointed out.

"Well, Dan doesn't get that way too often, and even when he does drink, something has to set him off."

"He had his eye on a girl at Lottie's last night, but he couldn't win her."

"And Andy did?"

I nodded.

"Well, Andy's his best friend," he said. "That girl must have really been something."

"Not really," I said. "She had these great big

knockers and these big dark eyes—"

"Diane!" he said. "Those eyes are really something, huh?"

"You too, huh?" I said.

"That gal has got eyes you could fall into and never find your way out of," he said, leaning close to me so he could whisper without his wife hearing him.

"Have you ever spent some time with her?" I asked.

"Not me," he said, straightening up. "I'm a happily married man." Then he grinned and said, "Besides, I'm a lousy poker player."

"That's no excuse, Jake," I said, putting my hand on his arm. "From what I saw last night, so are their dealers."

SEVENTEEN

I was sitting at a corner table nursing a beer when Andy Beauchamp walked in through the batwing doors with a friend.

It was Dan Dupree. Andy spotted me first and pointed me out to Dupree, who stared at me for a moment then started across the room towards me.

Dupree had a crumpled hat pulled down on his head, which looked like it was too big for his shoulders. It had not dawned on me the night before, but he very likely had the biggest head I've ever seen on a man. Like Jake Flynn, he wasn't that tall, but he was thick around the middle, with heavily muscled arms and legs, and hands that were probably as big as Flynn's.

There was a scowl on his face as he crossed the room and I pushed my chair back a bit, just in case I had to get up fast.

When he reached my table he planted his feet firmly and rumbled, "You are Clint Adams?" in a French accent.

"That's right."

"It was you who struck me on the head last night?"

"Yes—" I said, ready to explain why, but he

didn't give me a chance to.

"By God, *mon ami,* you gave me a good shot," he said, clapping one massive hand down on my shoulder. "My head still aches."

It took me a moment to realize that the expression on his face was supposed to be a smile.

"I'm glad you're all right," I said, conscious of the power that existed in the hand that was still holding my shoulder.

"I am fine," he assured me, banging on my shoulder once again. "It would take more than a bump on zee head to keep Dan Dupree down."

"I believe it," I said, moving my shoulder slightly to escape his grasp.

Andy Beauchamp came over at that moment and asked, "Are you two friends now?"

"*Oui,* we are good friends," Dupree said, pulling a chair out so he could sit. "We drink together."

"Is that a good idea?" I asked Andy, who also pulled out a chair.

"We'll watch him," Andy told me. "Jake, bring a bottle and three glasses."

Jake came over with the bottle and glasses and gave me the eye, and I shrugged.

"What did you do with your day today, my friend?" Andy asked as he poured three drinks.

I told him of my travels and my adventures, and when I mentioned going to Miss Lottie's house, his eyebrows went up and he said, "I am impressed with the company you keep."

"Don't be," I told him.

"She is beautiful, no?" he asked.

"She is beautiful, yes," I agreed, "but another cold woman I don't need."

"Another?"

I was thinking of Abby O'Shea, but I said, "Never mind."

We sat and finished the bottle, and I saw that Andy was pouring Dupree less and less each time, so that it was he and I who were consuming most of the whiskey.

When the bottle was gone Dupree stood up and said, "Well, I must go."

"Where?" I asked.

"To Miss Lottie's," Andy answered.

"The dark-eyed one," Dupree said, smiling.

"Didn't you have enough?" I asked him.

He grinned broadly, showing several gaps where teeth were missing and said, *"Mon ami,* a Frenchman never has enough. *Bon,* I will see you both later."

"Eh," Andy said, grabbing his wrist with one hand and pointing with the other. "Do not drink too much."

"Of course not," he said. "My eyes must be clear so that I can see my cards, no?"

"Don't raise," I told him. "The dealer has nothing to lose. Remember that."

"I will remember," he promised and, with a wave, was out the door.

"Will he be all right?" I asked.

"He'll be fine," Andy assured me. "He is like a big child, and I have scolded him. A child is always on his best behavior after he has been scolded," he explained.

"You sound like an expert on children," I said.

"I should be," he said. "I have three of my own."

"You have kids?" I asked, surprised.

He nodded and said, "In Ottawa."

"And a wife?"

He grinned sheepishly and said, "Yes, and a wife."

"What do they think about you being here, in the United States?" I asked.

"What is the difference to them," he asked, "whether I am here, or at Fort Macleod. Either way, I am not with them."

"Do they know you're in the U.S.?"

"Oh, yes, they know," he said. "I will see them . . . very soon, now. As soon as I have made enough money."

"When will that be?"

"Soon," he said, looking into the empty bottle. "Perhaps sooner than any of us thinks. I will get another bottle, eh?" he said, and went to the bar for it.

EIGHTEEN

When I got back to my hotel that night there was someone waiting for me in my room—which could have started to become annoying. At first I thought it was Abby again, but I was wrong.

It was Leticia.

"Well, well, Miss Lottie," I said, shutting the door behind me.

She got up from the bed and said, "I thought we settled that this morning. It's Leticia, Clint."

"Miss Lottie, Leticia," I said. "The question is still—what are you doing here?"

"You invited me," she said.

"I what?"

"You said that next time we talked, it should be here, remember?"

"I did say that, didn't I," I answered. "I hardly expected you to take me up on it . . . this soon, that is."

"The sooner, the better," she said, walking up to me. "I think we should get the amenities out of the way first, don't you?" she asked.

"And what would they be?" I asked.

She smiled and said, "Don't be deliberately dense, Clint. It doesn't suit you."

She was standing right in front of me now. She was almost as tall as I was, which was pretty damn tall for a woman. I hadn't noticed it that morning because she had remained seated the entire time.

She slid her arms around my neck easily and fitted her mouth to mine, opening it and probing with her tongue.

When she moved her mouth I said, "Does this come under the heading of amenities to you?"

"Of course."

"That's funny," I said. "To me this is the important part."

"Then perhaps I've put it badly," she said. "Let me try again. What I want is for us to become friends as soon as possible, so that we can really talk." She traced my lips with her tongue, and then said, "Is that better?"

"It'll do," I said. I began returning her kisses, then pushed her towards the bed. When the back of her knees struck the bed we tumbled down onto it and I let my weight bear down on her.

"I think we should get undressed first, don't you?" she asked.

"In a minute," I said.

I lay there on top of her, looking at her, and when I didn't move she started to get annoyed.

"Clint, let me up," she said tightly, then added in a different tone, "darling."

"I'm comfortable," I said, and it was then she realized what I was doing, that I was trying to see how far I could push her before she would drop the act.

"All right, god damn it, let me up then and we'll talk," she said, finally.

"Is that an order, Miss Lottie?" I asked.

"Yes," she snapped. Then, "No, damn it, it's a request. Please let me up."

"That's more like it," I said. I put my hands flat on the bed and lifted my weight off of her, then stood up. She looked as if she were waiting for me to offer to help her up, then she put her hand behind her and pushed herself to a seated position.

"You turned down a chance at a job without asking what the job was," she said. "That makes me curious."

"Why?"

"Do you have a job?" she asked.

"No."

"Are you wealthy?"

"No."

"And you don't need a job?"

"No."

"Wouldn't that make you curious?" she asked.

"Okay, so you're curious," I said. "I'll admit something. I'm curious, too."

"About the job?"

"No, about why you would ask a man you've never met to come to your house and then offer him a job."

"I thought you were right for it, judging from what I'd heard," she said.

"Heard from who?"

"People," she said, "who were in the Palace last night. You were good, last night, from all accounts. You knew how to play cards, you knew how to play my dealer, and then you took care of the big miner and two of my men without seriously injuring any of them."

"Didn't one of your men have a broken nose?" I asked.

"I don't consider that serious," she said. "I mean you didn't cripple anyone, or shoot anyone. You know how to handle yourself, and probably know how to use a gun, too."

"I told you that this morning," I said.

"So you did," She leaned forward and clasped her hands together in her lap. She was wearing a dress that probably cost more than everything I owned put together. It was high necked, but it hugged her, showing off the firm contours of her large, thrusting breasts. On the chair by the window was a fur jacket that must have cost even more than the dress.

"Clint, I need a man with your qualities to—"

"Stop right there, Leticia," I said, holding up my hand. "I'll tell you now that I don't care if you want me to deal for you, rob a bank for you, or be your partner in Lottie's—I'm not interested."

Her eyes widened, as if I had hit the nail right on the head. God knew, if that jerk last night was any indication, she could use some new dealers. Still, I wasn't interested in a job, and I didn't even know if I was interested in staying in Helena, Montana anymore.

There was, however, something I was interested in. After all, I was only a man, and she was a beautiful woman.

"Are you sure?" she asked.

"Well," I said, sitting on the bed next to her, "you could try to persuade me."

She smiled then, a triumphant smile, and I was glad she did. As I put my hand over one breast and squeezed it, I realized that I might have felt guilty about deceiving her had she not smiled that way. She felt that all she had to do now was sleep with me, and I'd be hers. She was that sure of her beauty and grace, and the control it gave her over men, all men.

"It unhooks in the back," she said. I kissed her then, and began to undo her dress. As I slipped it off of her I discovered that she had come prepared. She was wearing no undergarments, another sign of her complete confidence in herself.

Her breasts were like two overripe melons, with large, dusky nipples that were hardening beneath my palms.

She was like Abby O'Shea in that she intended to use sex to get what she wanted from me, but unlike Abby, she was enjoying it.

Her breath was already coming in short gasps and I could feel her heart beating in her breast. I kissed her and helped her off with her dress until she was totally naked. Goose bumps appeared on her smooth skin, but she didn't seem to notice. Perhaps they were more a result of excitement than of the cold.

"Are you cold?" I asked.

"Warm," she said, against my lips, "hot. Your turn. Take off your clothes."

When I'd removed my clothes, she ran her hand over my flesh and said, "You're cold. Come into bed with me and I'll warm you."

We crawled beneath the covers together, and she seemed to wrap herself around me. Her skin was incredibly hot—or maybe mine was that cold, but together we started to heat up.

Her mouth was crawling over mine, in moist, sweet kisses that had me rigid and ready—as she

soon found out. Her hand went down and I felt
her shiver as she touched that hard column between my legs.

"Marvelous," she sighed. "I'd love to play
with it, but I want it in me . . . now!"

She rolled over on her back, as if submitting to
me, but I knew that she thought that she was in
complete control. I climbed aboard her and eased
into the saddle, allowing myself to be swallowed up
slowly by her. She moaned and covered my mouth
with hers again, then kept on moaning against my
lips. Her legs came up and around me and I slid
my hands beneath her to cup her ass. At one point
she tried to move her behind, but I wouldn't let
her. I think that was when she first realized that
she was *not* in complete control.

"Let me—" she started to say, but I held her
tight and fast, not letting her move anyway or anywhere I didn't want her to.

"No," I said. "Let me."

She looked into my eyes and for a moment the
confidence faded and she looked confused. Then
I moved and suddenly her eyes seemed to go out
of focus, then she closed them, as she was over-
come by her passion, her pleasure.

I rotated her hips to match my tempo as I
eased myself in and out of her, slowly at first, and
then faster, until she was moaning and crying out
and I knew that I was in control, not her.

And she knew it, too.

"Don't—" she started to say, staring into my
eyes, and I think she wanted me to let up on her,
allow her to regain control of herself, but then even
that faded and she simply surrendered herself to
the sensations that were overcoming her.

I continued to grind myself into her, holding fast to her buttocks, keeping her pinned against me. She moved as I moved, with no further resistance, and then suddenly her entire body stiffened and she threw her head back, and then just as suddenly she was limp, as I started to empty myself into her.

I rolled off of her when I was spent, but she still did not move. She was conscious, so it was her choice too remin motionless, for some reason.

"I'm trying . . . to get used . . . to this," she said, as if reading my mind. Her words came haltingly as she fought to catch her breath.

"Used to what?" I asked.

"No man . . . has ever done that . . . to me before," she said, and she did not sound pleased.

"You didn't like it?" I asked.

She turned to me then as she said, "That's what takes getting used to. I loved it."

"You make that sound terrible," I said.

She moved her head again, this time so that she was staring at the ceiling.

"Not terrible," she said, "Just puzzling. I'll have to get used to it and then deal with it."

"You mean, make sure that it doesn't happen again?" I asked. "Make sure that you never lose control again?"

She sat up in bed then, threw back the sheet and swung her feet to the floor. She began to get dressed, her face expressionless. Fully dressed she looked at me again and said, "What makes you think I ever lost control?"

"Come on, Leticia," I said. "I know—"

"I may not have had complete control," she said, walking to the window to pick up her fur and wrap it around her. "But don't think that you ever did, either."

At the door she turned and said, "We'll talk again," and walked out.

NINETEEN

I admit, the coolness with which Leticia had walked out the night before had kept me awake for a short time, but once I convinced myself that she was only trying to save her pride, I fell right to sleep.

Well, almost right to sleep.

Waking the next morning, I still maintained to myself that no woman was *that* good an actress. No woman can deliberately make that look appear in her eyes. I was convinced of that.

Almost.

I was also convinced of one other thing, though, and that was that I had no further business staying in Helena. There was nothing to keep me there, and it was time to move on.

I got dressed and went out to breakfast, hoping to catch Andy Beauchamp before he went to work. I didn't know where he was living, so the only place I had to look for him was at Jake Flynn's saloon.

"Jake, has Andy Beauchamp been in for breakfast yet?" I asked as I walked in.

"Good morning to you, too, and no, he hasn't,"

he answered. "Who put a burr under your saddle?"

"Nobody," I said. "I'm just getting ready to leave and I'd like to say good-bye to him."

"You're pulling up stakes?" he asked. "So soon?"

"There are other places to see, Jake," I said, "but I won't leave until I have another one of your great breakfasts."

"You got it," he said, "and the last one's on the house."

"I won't argue with you there."

Jake brought the breakfast to my corner table, and I was almost done with it when Andy finally walked in. I waved him over to my table and he told Jake that he'd have breakfast.

" 'Morning," he said, sitting down.

"How did it go at Lottie's last night?" I asked. When I had started back to my room, Andy had gone on to Lottie's to see that Dan Dupree stayed out of trouble.

"Well, Dan still didn't win the dark-eyed girl, but we didn't get into a brawl, either," he said. "Must have had something to do with the fact that you weren't there," he added, kidding.

"Well, if that's the case, then you'll be glad to hear that I'm leaving, today."

"Already?"

"Time to go," I said. "There's nothing here to make me stay."

"What about Miss Lottie?" he asked. "And the other one, Abby O'Shea."

"I'll make you a gift of them both," I said. "You go and tell them that I recommended you for whatever job it was they had in mind for me."

He stared at me for a moment, then said, "That might not be a bad idea, but that still doesn't mean that I want you to leave."

"I appreciate that, Andy," I said. "I really do. But I've got to go."

"Do you know where you're going?"

"The Dakotas, probably. I've never been there, then I'll probably just head back south."

"You ever get tired of traveling?"

"Yeah, Andy, I do, sometimes," I said, "but then I look at the alternatives, and I've already been through that, too. So what's left?"

"I know where there are some openings for a Mountie or two," he said, and we both laughed.

Over breakfast—his, that is, since I'd finished mine—he said, "What would it take for you to stay?"

"Oh, something interesting, I guess," I said.

"Two job offers from beautiful women isn't interesting enough for you?" he asked.

"I said interesting, not suspicious."

"There you go with that suspicious mind again," he said.

"It's something I developed over the years, Andy," I said. "It's hard to get rid of, and since it's kept me alive from time to time, I don't think I want to."

"You leaving from here?" he asked, finishing up his food.

"I'll head back to the hotel and check out, then over to the livery and gone. My horse has probably forgotten what I look like."

"Come on," he said. "I'll walk you to the hotel

and then I'll get to work. Sure wish I had some cash stashed away."

"What for?"

"I'd buy a horse and ride along with you for a while," he said.

Andy was okay, but somehow I was glad he didn't have that much cash stashed away. When I travel—which is all the time—I like to do it alone.

"Take care, Jake," I said to Flynn. "Stay faithful to your wife."

A wide grin split his face and he said, "But of course, Clint."

We walked to the batwing doors and as we were about to go through Andy stopped short.

"Well, I'll be . . ." he said.

"What is it?" I asked.

"See those men riding down the street?" he asked.

I looked. There were five of them, looking as if they had ridden long and hard.

"The one in front is Jerry Potts," he said, "a guide for the Northwest Mounted Police. The man riding next to him is my commanding officer, Assistant Commissioner Macleod."

"The other three are Mounties?" I asked.

He nodded.

"I wonder what they're doing here," I asked, but Andy didn't answer. He was busy staring after them as they rode past, wondering the same thing.

"Hey, Jake," I called out.

"Yeah, Clint?"

"Set up a couple of beers, will you?" I said.

"For you and Andy?" Jake said.

"That's right," I said. I walked over to the bar, leaving Andy by the door.

"You ain't leaving?" he asked.

"Not yet," I said, reaching for my beer. "Something interesting just came up."

TWENTY

Andy finally walked away from the front doors and came over to get his beer.

"You think they're here for you and your friends?" I asked.

"What else?"

"I don't think so," I said.

He looked at me. "Why not?"

"You said there were about eighteen of you, if I remember correctly."

"That's right."

"Macleod wouldn't come for eighteen men with only four," I reasoned. "It wouldn't make sense."

"You know, you're right," Andy said. "But if that's the case, why *are* they here?"

"What have you been waiting for all this time?" I asked. "Hoping for?"

"You mean—"

I nodded.

"Maybe he's come to ask you all back . . . with back pay and all," I said. "There's only one way to find out."

"Ask him?"

I nodded again.

"All of you don't have to go. Just one of you."

"Which one?"

I shrugged.

"Pick a representative," I suggested. "Go see this assistant commissioner of yours and find out what he wants. What could that hurt?"

"Nothing," he agreed. Then he looked at me and said, "Will you do it?"

"Me?" I said in surprise. "Why me?"

"You could be an impartial, uh—"

"Go-between?"

"Yes, a go-between. I'm sure I could get the others to agree," he said.

"I don't know, Andy—"

"You said you would stay in town if something interesting came up," he said. "You also said that we were friends. I'm asking you to do me a favor, Clint. See what Macleod wants."

I frowned, wondering how I got myself into these things.

"All right," I said. "All right. Talk to the others, and if they agree, I'll go and see Macleod."

"That's great," he said. "Jake, another two beers, and then I'll go to work and talk to the others." He looked at me and said, "I know they'll go along with our plan."

"Our plan?" I asked.

"Well, we came up with it together, didn't we?" he said.

"Oh, sure," I said, picking up my beer. "Two great minds with a single thought."

I will say one thing for the arrival of Assistant Commissioner James Macleod in Helena, Montana, it did pique my interest enough to make me want to stay in town a little longer—at least until I found out what the story was.

There was another consideration as well. As an ex-lawman, I had been very interested to hear of the formation of the Northwest Mounted Police in 1873, and this was the first time I had ever come in contact with anyone who was connected with them.

The arrival of Macleod and his men was the something interesting I had needed to keep me in Montana—but the prospect of being able to *talk* to Macleod was *very* interesting.

TWENTY-ONE

Andy Beauchamp arranged a meeting of his fellow Mounties that evening in Jake Flynn's saloon, and I was invited to attend. Since most of the men were regular customers of Jake's, he made his back room available to us, and even supplied us with beer and liquor.

I arrived early, and Andy was there with his friends Robert and LeClerc, as well as Dan Dupree.

I pulled Andy aside and said, "Do you think we can keep Dan away from the liquor tonight? We'll need cool heads, here."

"We will take care of him, my friend," Andy assured me. "Don't worry. Dan is a big pussycat."

"Sure," I said.

I took a seat in a corner and watched as they filed in, one by one and two by two, until they were all there. Jake sent his wife back to take drink orders, and it was the first time I had gotten to see Mrs. Flynn. She was a large, stolid woman, about her husband's age, with a face that—if you wished to be kind—could have been called "pleasant."

Beer and whiskey were ordered, and then Andy stood up and quieted everyone down.

"Some of you still don't know why I called you here," he told them, "so I will explain."

He went on to tell them that he had seen Commissioner Macleod ride into town with Jerry Potts and three other men.

"So, we are here to decide what we are going to do," he finished up.

"If he has come for us, there are too many of us to hide," Robert said.

"I agree," Andy said. "But I for one would not even attempt to hide. Are we ashamed of what we have done?"

From the reaction to that question, there were a few men in the room—more than a few—who were.

"Well, I am not," Andy said. "My new friend, Clint Adams, has pointed something out, and I agree with it. The commissioner would not come for us with only four men. There must be another reason that he is here."

"What could that be?" LeClerc asked. The normally dour look on his face was even gloomier than usual.

"I propose that perhaps he is here to take us back," Andy said. "And I mean to *ask* us to come back, not to force us to."

A rumble began to work its way through the room as they discussed the possibility amongst themselves.

"How do we find out?" another man finally asked.

"That is obvious," a deep voice boomed out from the back of the room. They all turned to look at Dan Dupree, who said, "We must ask the commissioner."

"Dan is right," Andy said.

"All of us?" someone asked.

"Of course not," Andy said. "One man must go to the commissioner and find out why he is here, and why he has come himself."

"Then we must decide which one of us it is to be," Robert said, and the others indicated their agreement.

"I have an idea about that," Andy said, and I told him to take all of the credit for it, even though we had "both" thought of it. "I think Clint Adams should go and talk to him for us."

"Why him?" someone asked.

"Because he is my friend—" Andy said, and he was cut off by Dan Dupree's voice as the big man boomed out, "And mine!"

"—and he has agreed to do it, if we all agree."

"Why should he do this for us?" asked another man.

"You should ask him that," Andy said, looking over at me and that was my cue to stand up.

"As Andy has said, he and I have become friends, but aside from that, I can't blame you men for doing what you did. It was asking a lot of you all to stay in the service, even though you had not been paid for six months. I would like to do what I can to help you."

"You do not expect to be paid?" a voice called out. I didn't see who had asked that question, but I stopped Andy before he could answer.

"I think it's a fair question, Andy," I said.

"I do not," he said, but remained silent after that.

"No, I don't expect any pay for doing this," I answered. "I was a lawman for a long time, and I look forward to meeting Commissioner Macleod and learning about the Northwest Mounted Police."

"I accept Climt Adams," Robert spoke up.

"I do, also," Dan Dupree said. He stood up holding a bottle of whiskey and added, "And I will break zee neck of any man who does not agree."

That sort of clinched it, and I was unanimously accepted.

"You do good job!" Dupree came over and told me, slapping me on the back hard enough to loosen the bullets in my gunbelt.

"I'd better," I said, taking the whiskey bottle from him and drinking from it.

TWENTY-TWO

The first step was to find out what hotel Macleod and his men had registered in. I figured that my hotel would be beneath the dignity of the Mounties, but by the same token, if they hadn't paid their men in six months—or at least, the men of Fort Macleod—they would not be staying in the most expensive hotel in town, either.

To avoid walking from hotel to hotel in Helena—I didn't even know how many there were—I asked Jake Flynn if he might not be able to find out for me. The meeting had broken up, and the Mounties had gone off to the various saloons.

"Where are you gonna be?" Flynn asked.

"Right over there," I said, pointing to the corner table I had taken up residence at since arriving in Helena. Andy Beauchamp was already sitting there, with Robert, LeClerc and Dan Dupree.

"I'll do what I can," he said. "You want a bottle over there?"

"Yes, but wait until Dupree leaves," I suggested. I knew that Dan was planning on going over to Lottie's to try for that dark-eyed girl again, so Jake nodded and I went over to the table and

103

took the empty chair they had left for me, the one against the wall.

As I sat, big Dan Dupree stood up and said, "Well, I go. Zee dark-eyed girl waits for me."

I saw a signal pass between Andy and Robert, and Robert and LeClerc also stood.

"We'll come with you," Robert said.

"To keep me out of trouble, no?" he asked, grinning widely.

"To keep you out of trouble, yes," Andy said.

"Ah, my friends," Dupree said, putting one massive arm around each man, and they marched that way from the saloon. As they left, Jake came over with a bottle and two glasses.

"So, what will you do now?" Andy asked, pouring out the whiskey.

"I've got Jake trying to find out what hotel Macleod is staying in," I said. "When he does, I'll go over and see him."

"What will you tell him?"

"The truth," I said. "I don't think it's any secret that you're here, right? I'll tell him that you're all concerned about why he's in town. I think he'll accept that you have every right to be—if he's as fair a man as you say he is."

"Oh, he is fair," Andy said, "but he is still an officer."

We clinked glasses on that, and drank.

A short time later I went back to my hotel and was only half relieved to find that no one was waiting for me in my room. I hung my gunbelt on the bedpost and lay down fully dressed on the bed. I was too tired and too cold to try undressing and getting under the covers before the chill hit.

I couldn't have been asleep more than a half an

hour when I was awakencd by a knocking on my door. I had left the lamp burning, and called out, "Coming" as I pushed myself to my feet.

As I stood up, I heard the glass in my window shatter, and then heard the report of the shot. I hit the floor, realizing that someone was shooting at me from a distance away, with a rifle.

I grabbed my gun from my gunbelt and rolled over to the window. I started to peek above the sill when there was another shot. I saw the muzzle flash from across the street before ducking back down.

With my lamp lit there wasn't much chance of my moving around without getting shot at, so I turned and snapped off a shot, shattering the lamp and plunging the room into darkness.

Now I peered above the sill again, trying to see through the darkness to the roof across the street. The street lamps were more a hindrance than a help. The rooftop across the way was higher than the lamps, and their light did not extend that far. If it had been pitch black out, I would have had a better chance of seeing.

I moved back towards the bed and pulled off the blanket and the pillow. Back at the window I propped them up on a chair, then placed my hat on top. I hoped it would fool the rifleman for just long enough for me to pinpoint his location.

I settled back onto the floor, took out a match and scraped it against the wall, lighting it. I peeked over the sill from the bottom left-hand corner of the window, waiting for whoever it was to fire another shot, but the sniper had apparently been discouraged by his two misses.

Cautiously, I stood up, but still there was no

third shot. The match burned down and I put it out and lit a second one.

I remembered the knock on the door and went to answer it, although I didn't expect to find anyone there. I wasn't disappointed. I stepped out into the hall and looked both ways, but there was no one in sight. Obviously, the knock had been to awaken me and cause me to stand up, giving the man a clear shot through the window. Luckily, the man behind the rifle had not been up to the task.

The second match burned my finger and I cursed and dropped it. I debated going down to the desk for an extra lamp, but decided against it. I went back into the darkened room, and after hanging an extra blanket over the broken window, to cut down on the draft, I lay back down on the bed. I didn't anticipate a second try, but I slept with my gun close at hand, just in case.

I fell asleep wondering what the hell I had done since arriving in town that would make someone want to kill me.

TWENTY-THREE

When I woke up the next morning, I realized that if I had left the day before, as I'd intended, I wouldn't have been shot at last night. Having been shot at now, there was no chance of my leaving until I found out who and why.

If it had been the shooter's intention to scare me out of town, he had done exactly the opposite, and he would regret it.

That is, they would regret it. It was obvious that whoever had knocked on my door had been in on it.

I stood up, washed my face in the washbasin and didn't even bother to change clothes. I strapped on my gun and went downstairs to talk to the desk clerk.

"Hey," I called out while still on the steps.

"What?" he asked, awakened from a half doze by my voice. I wondered if this clerk did his sleeping and eating behind the desk. There hadn't been a time since I checked in when I didn't see him behind it.

"Is your name Deke Manson?" I asked, remembering that was who the sheriff had said owned the place.

"That's right."

So he was the owner as well as the clerk, and if I was his only guest, he sure as hell couldn't afford to hire someone else.

"After I came in last night, did anyone else come in?" I asked.

"I wish they had, mister," he said. "I could use another guest."

"I'm not talking about another guest," I said. "I'm talking about anybody at all."

"Well, nobody that I saw," he said, scratching the stubble on his chin. "Why?"

"Somebody knocked on my door last night."

"Who were it?"

"I don't know," I said. "When I got up to answer it, somebody took a shot at me through the window."

His eyes widened and he said, "Did they break my winder?"

"No, I'm fine, thanks," I said, dryly. "You didn't hear a shot last night?"

"Mister, when I'm full asleep, I don't hear nothing, and I was full asleep after you went upstairs."

"Then somebody could have come in without you seeing them?" I asked.

"That's what I said," he answered. "Nobody came in that I saw."

"You're a big help. Have you got any extra kerosene lamps?"

"Why? What's the matter with the one in your room?" he asked.

"Somebody shot it out," I told him.

"They broke my lamp, too?" he cried out.

"I'm afraid so."

"God damn it!" he snapped. "I ain't got no money to be repairing windows and lamps."

"Well, I'm going to need another room," I said. "With that window pane shattered, it's just like sleeping outside."

"I'll move you into room eight," he said without argument.

"Don't bother," I said. "I'll move myself when I come back from seeing the sheriff."

"You going to see the sheriff?" he asked.

"Isn't that what you usually do when someone takes a shot at you?" I asked. "Report it to the law?"

"I reckon," he said. "Would you tell him that someone broke a window and a lamp on me, too? If he catches the varmint, mebbe he can get him to pay for the damage."

If that were the case, I doubted that he'd use the money to fix the broken window and lamp, anyway.

"Yeah, I'll tell him," I said. I was about to leave and then turned back and said, "And listen, stop letting people go up into my room, will you?"

"You talking about them two, ah, ladies?"

"Have you let anyone else up?"

"Just the ladies," he said with a knowing look. "Can't see why you'd be complaining."

"I happen to like my privacy," I said. "Or would you rather I take my business to another hotel."

"Now there ain't no need for that kind of talk," he said. "Don't you worry none, mister, ain't nobody going to go into your room less'n you let them in yourself."

"I hope not."

"Ah, you wouldn't be wanting to settle your bill up to now, would you?" he asked.

"Why would I?"

"Ah, well, I was just thinking. Seeing as how somebody took a shot at you last night, it could just happen again today. You wouldn't want to die with unpaid bills, now would ya?"

I stared at him for a long moment until he lowered his eyes and said, "Well, it was just a suggestion."

"I'm touched by your concern," I said. "Remember, nobody goes in my room."

"I'll remember," he said. "I swear."

"And in the future," I said, "keep your suggestions to yourself. I'm not in the mood for them."

"Yes, sir. Glad you wasn't hurt none, sir."

"Oh, shut up," I told him, and got out of there.

TWENTY-FOUR

When I walked into the sheriff's office he looked up from shining his boots and said, "What do you want?"

His attitude made me even angrier than I already was.

"I just wanted you to know that while you were making sure you had a fine shine on your boots, somebody took a couple of shots at me last night in my hotel room."

"Got to watch what kind of whores you takes into your room," he said. "Some of them carry guns."

"Sheriff, somebody took two shots at me from the roof across the street from my hotel."

"I guess they missed," he said. "So what do you want me to do about it?"

"Well, for starters, you could go up on that roof and see if you can find any spent shells."

"What would that tell me?" he asked. "That the rifle fired forty-four or forty-five caliber slugs? What would you want me to do then? Arrest anyone carrying the same caliber?"

"I want you to do your job," I said.

He gave me a sharp look then and put down the boot he was working on.

"Don't come to my town and try to tell me how to do my job, Adams," he said. "You might have been a lawman once, but you ain't no more, so you talk to me with respect."

"A badge gets respect automatically, Sheriff," I told him. "But a man has got to earn it."

I didn't wait for his reply, but got out of there before I said or did something one of us would be sorry for.

TWENTY-FIVE

I decided to get a look at that rooftop myself. If the shooter had been in a hurry to get away, he might have left something helpful behind.

From out in front of my hotel, I could pinpoint the roof the sniper must have been on. What I discovered surprised me: the rooftop that he had to have been on was part of Miss Lottie's. He hadn't been standing directly over the big yellow sign, which was why it hadn't been obvious at first, but now that I was looking at it in the daylight, I was sure that was where he had been.

I went over to Jake Flynn's to see if he had any information for me yet on the whereabouts of Commissioner Macleod, and also to digest what I had discovered so far about the shooting.

" 'Morning, Jake," I said.

"Breakfast?" he asked.

"Information."

"I'll give it to you with breakfast."

"You got a deal," I said, and went to my table.

A few minutes later he brought over a pot of coffee and a plate of food and sat down with it.

"That fella you're looking for is staying at the Helena House Hotel," he said.

"Sounds expensive," I said. "Is that the best hotel in town?"

"No," he answered. "There's another one in town called the Montana House. That's the most expensive place in town. You're right about the Helena House, though, it does sound expensive, but that's as close as it gets."

"Okay," I said. "That's like I figured. Thanks, Jake."

"Do I get to know what this is all about?" he asked. I was sure he had some idea, but I thought it should be up to Andy and the rest of them if they wanted to fill him in on the whole thing.

"Ask Andy, Jake," I said. "It would be up to him to fill you in, or not."

"Fair enough," he said, standing up. As he did, Andy Beauchamp came walking in and Jake said, "Speak of the devil."

"Tell the Missus to whip me up a big one, Jake," Andy said, coming over to the table. "This is going to be an interesting day, I think."

"You got it," Jake said.

Andy sat down and asked, "Did you find out where the commissioner is staying?"

"I did," I said, "and I'll talk to him today. Something else has come up, though, Andy." I told him about the incident from the night before and he rubbed his jaw thoughtfully as he listened.

"Why would anyone want to shoot at you?" he asked when I'd finished.

"There are a lot of people who'd want to shoot at me, Andy," I told him. "But none that I know of are in this town."

"What do you think it was about, then?"

"I don't have any idea," I said. "The only

thing I'm involved in right now is talking to Macleod for you and the others."

"Why would anyone want to shoot at you because of that?" he asked. "You're doing us a favor."

"I don't know, Andy," I said, "but I'm going to find out."

Jake came over with a large breakfast for Andy, who immediately went to work on it.

"How did Dan make out last night?" I asked.

"Still no luck, but he isn't finished trying."

"Did you keep him out of trouble?"

"He didn't break anything, if that's what you mean," he said. "Listen, do you think they'll let you go up on the roof at Miss Lottie's to look around?"

"I don't know what I'm going to ask," I said. "Maybe I'll just go over there tonight for some fun."

"You mean, take one of the girls upstairs, and then go and look at the roof?" he asked. I nodded, and he said, "You've got to win one of them, first."

"We'll see what we can do about that," I said.

"I better come along, just to keep you out of trouble," he suggested.

"You mean like last time?"

"Now that was your own fault," he reminded me. "Remember, you took the blame.

"Well, not all of it," I said. "But okay, I'll still accept most of it. Tonight, however, I'll just be another customer, and if I should get lucky, I'll be just as happy as anyone else."

"You going to try for Diane?" he asked.

The thought had crossed my mind, in fact.

"I might, if you'll help," I said.

"What?"

I leaned over and speared a piece of ham from his plate and said, "Do something about keeping Dan out of there tonight. I got lucky last time. The last thing I want to do is tangle with him again."

"It's a deal," he said, "and if you're still hungry, get some more breakfast and keep your hand off mine."

"I thought we were friends," I said. "Share and share alike."

"Everything but food," he said, "and women."

TWENTY-SIX

The Helena House was a decent hotel, though obviously not a very expensive one. It was three stories high, but was in a slightly rundown condition, which no first-rate hotel would allow to happen.

I presented myself to the desk clerk and said, "I'd like to see a James Macleod."

The clerk looked me over, then checked his registration book.

"Would that be Commissioner Macleod, sir?" he asked.

"Yes, that's him."

"He's in room three-oh-three, sir—"

"Thank you."

"—but I don't think he's in at the moment," he went on, ignoring my interruption.

"Would you know where he is?" I asked.

"I believe he's having breakfast in the hotel dining room," he said, "with the rest of his party." He pointed to a doorway over which there was a sign that said Dining Room.

"All right," I said. "Thank you."

"Of course, sir," he answered, and went back to his work.

I went over to the doorway and looked into the dining room. The room was large and had a faded charm that told me that, some time ago, it might have been the most expensive hotel in town.

I saw the group Andy had pointed out to me the day before seated at a large table, all eating breakfast. As I approached the table, Jerry Potts, the scout, looked up and we locked eyes. Even then, he was scouting for Macleod. He said something to the others, who also looked up, and they both watched me as I continued walking up to them.

"Commissioner Macleod?" I asked.

"That's right," he answered. "Do I know you, sir?" His accent was very different from Andy's and Dan Dupree's. Definitely not French. It struck me that this man spoke English as I had never heard it before. Clear, precise, every word achieving its full potential.

"No, you don't," I answered. "My name is Clint Adams. I wonder if we might talk for a few minutes . . . alone."

He regarded me for a moment, obviously deciding whether or not he did want to talk to me, and then he looked at each of the other men in turn. His three troopers all rose at once, took their plates, and moved to another table. Jerry Potts didn't move right away, and Macleod looked at him and said, "It's all right, Potts."

"Yes, sir," Potts said, and then he picked up his plate and moved to the table with the others.

"Sit down, sir," Macleod invited me. He was a good-looking man, with a full head of brown hair, muttonchops and a beard. Can I offer you some coffee?"

"Yes, thank you," I said. He graciously poured

it for me, then sat back in his chair and said, "Now, suppose you tell me just what it is you want to talk to me about."

"It's about your men, sir," I said. The "sir" came out by itself, because the man seemed to command respect.

"My men?" he asked. "What about my men?"

"I'm referring to the eighteen or so who deserted and came to Montana," I said.

He laughed shortly and said, "Who told you such a preposterous story, Mr. Adams?"

"They did, sir," I answered.

I could understand where the Mounties would not want to admit that such a thing had happened, but I hoped to be able to convince him that I was indeed acting for them. If I wasn't, then one of them would end up having to speak to him, anyway.

"I'm afraid you've been rather misinformed, Mr. Adams," Macleod said, "and I would now like to finish my breakfast in peace."

"Excuse me, sir," I said, "but if you will let me have my say, perhaps I can convince you that there's no need to pretend that the incident never occurred."

He thought about it and then said, "Very well, then, have your say, so that I may get on with my breakfast."

"Thank you," I said.

I explained why I had been chosen to come and speak to him on their behalf, and mentioned a couple of names that I had been assured he would recognize.

Following my explanation he took his time digesting the information and finishing his breakfast.

I didn't push him, because I wanted him to decide in my favor.

"Mr. Adams," he finally said, "I don't see how I can divulge to you the reason for my presence here without some . . . evidence that what you say is true."

"I thought perhaps the names I gave you—" I started to say, but he cut me off simply by shaking his head.

"I'm afraid that won't do," he said.

"Do you admit, then, that you are here because of these men?" I asked.

"I don't admit—as yet—that these men exist, but if you should happen to come back with one of them, then perhaps we could talk again," he said.

"The point of my coming to see you—"

He held up a hand to silence me this time, and said, "I know what the point of your coming was, Mr. Adams." He hesitated a moment, then made a small concession and said, "If there *are* some of my men in this town, I am certainly not here to do them any harm."

"I'll relay that message," I said.

"If there are any here," he reminded me.

"Of course."

"If you should happen to come back with a friend," he said, "I'll instruct the desk to let you come up to my room."

I stood up and said, "Thank you, Commissioner."

"Thank you, Mr. Adams," he said. "I look forward to talking to you again, when we can do so more freely."

Neither one of us offered to shake hands. I nodded to him and turned to leave, finding myself face to face with Jerry Potts.

"You about done, Commissioner?" he asked.

"Mr. Adams was just leaving, Potts," Macleod said.

"Well, I just wanted to remind you that we have to get to the bank and—"

"Potts!" Macleod snapped, and Potts's mouth closed like a bear trap.

Macleod and I exchanged glances at that point, and I knew that not another word would pass between them until I left, so I said, "Good day, Commissioner," and left.

TWENTY-SEVEN

"The bank?" Andy asked, later that evening.

"That's what Potts said, but Macleod shut him up pretty quick," I said. "He's a careful man, this commissioner of yours."

"Do you see what this means?" he asked.

"What?"

"Well, what do people go to a bank for?"

"To rob it," I suggested, kidding.

"Besides that," he said. "They go there for money."

"You think the Mounties have put together a payroll?"

"And the Commissioner is here to ask us to come back."

"That's possible," I said, "but somebody has to come with me next time I talk to him."

"I will," he said.

"On second thought, maybe you should just go alone. The original idea was for me to go so none of you would have to. Now if you have to go anyway, what's the point of having me along?"

"Because you are my friend, and I would like you to come," he said.

"Well," I said, "when you put it that way, how can I resist?"

"You cannot," he said, looking puzzled.

"That's what I meant," I said.

"Oh."

We were in Flynn's, just the two of us, seated at the same table as always, and now I said, "Look, finish your drink because I want to get over to Miss Lottie's."

"Still want to get a look at that rooftop," he said.

"Uh-huh."

"Do you really hope to find anything?" he asked.

"I'm keeping an open mind," I said. "Once I doused the light in my room he might have taken off quickly enough to leave something behind without meaning to."

"That does not seem very likely to me," he said.

I frowned, wondering why he was trying to talk me out of it, and said, "Likely or not, I'm going up there on that roof. You don't have to come along if you don't want to."

"I have nothing else to do tonight," he said.

"Then let's go," I said. "The sooner I get up there the better chance I have of finding something."

TWENTY-EIGHT

When we walked into Miss Lottie's I got a dirty look from a bouncer who I didn't recognize, but who apparently recognized me. He didn't have a broken nose, so he must have been the other man I hit that night.

"Good evening," I said to him.

"I'm going to be watching you real close to-night, friend," he said, "and I hope you start something."

"Well, there's always hope," I said. "Come on, Andy."

"You going to play now, Clint?" he asked.

"Maybe we'll get a drink first and look the tables over," I said. "I don't really want to play the same dealer as the other night, but maybe we can find another one just as easy."

We walked to the bar where I ordered two beers. I looked around and saw that, although most of the girls in the place were assigned certain tables, there were a few of them walking around free.

I was surprised to find that one of them was the dark-eyed girl, Diane.

She noticed me at the same time I noticed her and started to walk over.

"Uh, Andy, why don't you mingle a bit," I said, "and keep your eye out for Dan Dupree."

"Don't worry about him," Andy said. "Robert and LeClerc are keeping him busy tonight."

"Just the same, go for a walk, all right?"

He looked at me, puzzled, and was about to speak when he saw the dark-eyed girl approaching, and understood.

"Oh, I see," he said. "I'll talk to you later."

"Sure."

As he walked away she approached and said, "Hello there."

"Hi."

"Come back for another round?" she asked.

"Of drinks?" I asked. "I didn't have any—"

"No, I meant like fights," she said, holding up her small fists.

"Oh, that," I said. "No, that was an unfortunate incident and one I'm not looking forward to repeating."

"Yeah, it was unfortunate," she said. "I kind of feel responsible for it, too."

"You? Why?"

"Well, after all, those were my chips that started the whole thing," she said. "Can I buy you a drink, to make up for it?"

"You want to buy me a drink?" I said.

"Sure, why not."

Her face was thin, with prominent cheekbones, and except for her large breasts, the rest of her body was thin as well. The outstanding feature, however, was undeniably her eyes.

"Aren't you working a table tonight?" I asked.

"Some nights we work the floor," she said, "like tonight."

"Well, if you really want to buy me a drink—" I said, turning to call for the bartender.

She put her hand on my arm and said, "Not here. I meant up in my room."

"Upstairs," I repeated, and she nodded, smiling. "Well, I'll tell you, Diane, I have this little unwritten rule for myself."

"Really? What is it?"

"I never pay for my pleasure," I said.

"Well, who said anything about paying?" she said. "After all, you did win me the other night."

"Yeah, but I don't have the chips anymore," I pointed out.

"That's okay," she said, taking my almost empty glass from me and putting it down on the bar. "I'm still willing to honor them. What do you say?"

"How could I turn down such a gracious offer?" I replied.

TWENTY-NINE

For such a skinny girl, her breasts were marvelously rounded and firm, with very large, brown nipples.

"Do you like them?" she asked as I nibbled on her breasts.

"Very much," I said.

We were both naked on the bed in her room, which was on the third floor. It was her private room, she said, and not the one where she took her "customers."

"You're not just another customer," she told me. "When I saw the way you handled those men the other night, it just got me so excited. I don't think I've been that excited before," she said. Then she added, "Or this excited."

She grabbed my head and pulled my face into her breasts, then reached between us to fondle my cock while I continued to bite her nipples and breasts.

"Oh God, mister . . ." she said as I sucked her nipples to their hardest.

She wiggled away from me then and slid down the bed until her face was nestled between my legs. I knelt there above her as she guided me into her mouth and began to work on me expertly.

She knew every time I was about to come, and she stopped me every time, and then continued on. Finally, when I thought I wouldn't be able to stand it any longer, she released me and wiggled back up underneath me.

"Put it in me, mister," she said. "Put it all the way in!"

I did just as she asked, driving myself home, and she squealed as I entered her roughly.

"Oh yes, mister, that's it, do it like that," she said as I proceeded to pump into her ruthlessly.

She kept her eyes open the whole time and there was something about staring into those bottomless, dark eyes that made this more than just an act of sex. I reached beneath her and took her slender, tight buttocks in my hands and pulled her against me.

There were times as we went on when I wanted to close my eyes, but I couldn't. Staring into her eyes like that, I was virtually unable to close my own. She began to do something with her hips that created new sensations, and then she began to fondle me with her hands, creating even more.

I held her so tightly that I thought I might hurt her, but she proved to be considerably stronger than she appeared. At last her body stiffened, and she lifted us both up off the bed as she climaxed—something a whore is not especially known for doing. But this was her own room, as she said, and here she was letting herself go, allowing herself to feel.

Then she made a small move that virtually yanked my orgasm from me, and still our eyes remained locked, even when I would have liked to squeeze mine tightly shut.

"Mmm, mister, that was so good," she said, stretching beneath me while I was still inside of her, semi-erect.

I didn't answer right away, mainly because I was a little out of breath, myself.

"You wanna stay the night, or what?" she asked.

"Wouldn't that get you in trouble?" I asked. "I mean, spending the night with someone and not coming out of it with any money."

"I make enough in a week to throw in a freebee or two," she assured me. "I'm real good, you know."

"Yes," I said, "I know. Do you like it here, Diane?"

"What?" she said, as if she couldn't believe I'd asked that. That was a "customer's" regular question. Do you like doing this, how did you get into this, and so on, but I was asking because I wanted to know. I had something in mind.

"No, I really mean it," I said. "I have a reason for asking."

"Don't they all?"

"I'm serious," I said.

"No, I don't like it here, but what's that got to do with anything?" she asked. "Do you think those miners like being in the mines? It's a job, that's all."

"And you don't feel any loyalty to the people who employ you here?" I asked.

"No, not especially," she said after a moment. "Why you asking all these questions?"

"I'll tell you the truth," I said, and then did. I told her about being shot at last night, and that I was sure that the shots came from the roof of Miss Lottie's, then I told her that I had come there this evening to try and get up on the roof to take a look.

"Look for what?"

"I won't know that until I get up there," I said.

"And you want me to get you up there?"

"You don't have to get involved," I said. "What if you fell asleep and I slipped out and went up? You couldn't get into trouble for that, could you?"

"I suppose not," she admitted. "So you don't want me to do anything except not give you away?"

"Exactly," I said.

She thought it over for a moment, then shrugged and said, "I don't suppose there's any harm in that, especially if someone was trying to kill you last night. I'd want to know who it was if it was me they took a shot at."

"Good," I said, getting up from the bed. "I really appreciate this, Diane."

As I dressed I asked her, "How will you explain bringing me up here instead of to the second floor?"

"Oh, that's no problem," she assured me. "It's not against the rules or anything to bring someone up here, it's just not done all that often."

She propped herself up on one elbow to watch me dress, and the sheet fell away, revealing one large, almost plump breast.

"You have incredible eyes, did you know that?" I asked.

"Yes, I know it," she said, "but it's nice to hear that from a man who means it. Thank you."

"You're welcome," I said.

I finished dressing, then reached into my pocket to take out some money.

"Hey, I thought you said you never paid for your pleasure," she reminded me.

"I don't," I said, laying the money on her dressing table. "This is to help you explain why you brought me up here, just in case anyone asks. It's not for what happened up here between you and me."

She smiled and said, "All right. Will you come back here afterward?"

"I doubt it," I said.

"Will you come back at all?"

I paused at the door and said, "Maybe. I can't promise anything."

She smiled again, wider this time, and bared her other breast, saying, "I can."

THIRTY

There wasn't much activity on the upper floor during business hours, because all of the girls were downstairs, on either the first or second floor, tending to business. That was lucky for me, because I didn't run into a soul while I was looking for a stairway to the roof.

Finally I found a door that opened onto a stairway and took it up to the roof. It was a dark, moonless night, and I took a moment to allow my eyes to adjust. When I was able to make out enough shapes so that I wouldn't trip over anything, I moved about looking for the side that overlooked the street where my hotel was.

I had left the lamp burning in my room, and since I was the only guest, there was no problem in picking it out.

The street was wide, and the rooftop was higher than my hotel room, but I had known men who could have put out a candle at that distance, striking flame and not the wax. Whoever had shot at me was not even good enough to hit a man at that distance—if indeed he had been trying to hit me.

I lit three or four matches and searched the immediate area for spent shells, or anything else that might help me find out who the gunman was, but nothing had been left behind. That led me to believe that the man had not hastily fled after firing, but that he had done precisely what he'd intended to, and then made damned sure that he didn't leave anything behind. He had deliberately missed, in an attempt to scare me.

I leaned my elbows on the roof ledge and looked down into the street. I decided that what I had to do now was find out who was threatened by my being in town, and I had to wonder what that person would try next, now that they hadn't succeeded in scaring me away.

I made a circuit of the roof, trying to find a way down other than going through the building. In the back there was another roof about one floor lower that the sniper could have dropped down to. I did so, in order to investigate further.

The roof I was now on sloped downward, and I followed to a point where I saw that it was possible to drop to the ground. I did that as well, and although it jarred my ankles, I received no lasting injury and proved that it could be done. It was probably also possible for him to have gained access to the roof of Miss Lottie's in the same manner.

I went back to my hotel with intentions of putting out the lamp I'd left in my old room, but decided to leave it lit. When I went to my new room, I raised the lamp only enough so that I could see, then hung my gunbelt on the bedpost and lay on the bed.

My last waking thought was that perhaps my name was not as unknown in Montana as I had thought. Maybe someone wanted to kill me not because I was a threat, but simply because I was "The Gunsmith."

THIRTY-ONE

I was awakened the next morning by someone knocking on my door. Sleepy as I was, I almost stood up immediately to answer it, but I caught myself and waited to see if there would be a second knock. I was sliding my gun from my holster when a voice called out, "Come on, Clint, it is only me, Andy Beauchamp."

"Andy," I said, but I didn't allow that to make me careless. Still holding my gun, I slipped from the bed and cautiously moved towards the door and let him in.

"Do you sleep with that?" he asked, looking at the gun in my hand.

"I keep it close," I said. "In case of emergency."

"Like the other night."

"Exactly." I walked to the bedpost and replaced the gun in the holster.

"So tell me what happened last night. You never came down after you went up with Diane."

"I used another route to come down," I said. I told him about going up to the roof and finding nothing, except for another way down.

"Yes," he said, "but what happened with the girl? Was she any good?"

I stared at him, then said, "A gentleman never tells, Andy. You should know that."

"Bah," he said, good-naturedly. "Are you ready to go and talk to Commissioner Macleod?"

"You just woke me up," I said. "Go over to Jake's and order breakfast for us, I'll meet you there after I change."

"All right," he said. "I don't mind telling you that I'm a little nervous."

"You have a right to be," I said. "Go on, I won't be very long," I promised.

He left and I used the washbasin to clean myself up, and then put on some fresh clothes. It wouldn't do to go and see the Commissioner in clothing I had slept in.

When I got to the saloon Jake was just serving breakfast.

"Just in time," he said.

Over breakfast Andy said, "So tell me what assumptions you have made after last night."

I told him everything, except what I thought about the attempt on me having something to do with my reputation.

"I still do not see what you could have done since you arrived in town to threaten anyone," he said.

"Well, there was the gambler, Gates," I said.

"But he's gone."

"And the dealer at Lottie's."

"I doubt that very much," he said. "I don't think that man has ever had anything more lethal than a deck of cards in his hands."

"All right," I said. "There were the two job offers I turned down. One from Abby O'Shea, and the other from Miss Lottie."

"Would they want to kill you just for turning down a job?" he asked.

"I admit that it doesn't sound very likely," I said, "but who else is there?"

"Well, certainly not any of us," he said, speaking of the Mounties. "You're trying to help us, and I think we all appreciate that fact."

"Are you sure?"

"Well, there may be some who don't want to go back," he admitted.

"Do they like it in the mines?" I asked.

"No, but neither do they relish going back into the wilderness, with only their own imaginations and each other for company."

"We still have to hear what Macleod is doing here before we assume that," I said.

"Then I suggest we do that now," he said.

"I agree." I lifted the coffeepot and added, "Right after one more cup of coffee."

THIRTY-TWO

"Oh, yes," the desk clerk at the Helena House said, after we'd given him our names. "You're expected, gentlemen. Go right up."

Jerry Potts answered the door, opening it wide, and staring first at me, then at Andy Beauchamp.

"Hello, Beauchamp."

"Potts," Andy said. "We're here to see the commissioner.

"I know," Potts answered. "Come on in."

We walked in and he shut the door behind us. The room was three times as large as mine and had the same faded class that the dining room had. There was a writing desk there, and Macleod was seated at it.

He stood up and said, "Hello, Andy, good to see you."

A change came over Andy Beauchamp. He held his hat in his hand, crumpled up and unnoticed, as he said, "Yes, sir. Good to see you too, sir."

"Mr. Adams," Macleod said, greeting me as well.

"Good morning," I said.

"Andy, I'm glad you've come to see me," Macleod said. "Why don't you both sit down?"

We settled into two straightbacked chairs, and I gave Andy a look of encouragement.

"Sir," Andy began, his eyes somewhere on Macleod's chest, as if he couldn't meet the man's eyes, "before we start, I'd like you to know that there wasn't anything personal in what we did—"

"Of course not," Macleod said, cutting him off. "I never thought there was, Andy. I understand how unhappy the men were. My God, I'm surprised that even more men didn't go with you."

"You are, sir?" Andy asked, surprised.

"Mr. Adams," Macleod said, drawing me into the conversation, "would you stay on a job for six months without getting paid?"

"I don't think so," I said, wary about giving my opinion.

"There, you see?" Macleod said to Andy. "So don't go worrying that I took anything personally, lad."

"Thank you, sir," Andy said. "That makes me feel a lot better."

"Well, then," the commissioner said. "Now that we've got that out of the way, let's get down to the business at hand, shall we?"

"Yes, sir."

"Mr. Adams, I think if you would care to wait outside—"

I was surprised that Andy spoke up when he did.

"Uh, sir, I think I would prefer to have Clint stay in the room. After all, he did agree to represent us—"

"For which he was paid, I assume," Macleod said. "I don't see where that gives him the right—"

"No, sir," Andy said. "Begging your pardon, but he wouldn't accept any payment."

"He wouldn't?" Macleod said, looking at me in a new light. "That's odd, isn't it?" he asked, and I didn't know if he was asking Andy or me.

"I don't believe it is, sir," I answered. "I had my own reasons for doing it."

"I'm sure you must have had some reason," Macleod said, "and I would be interested in hearing what it was . . . after we complete our business." He looked at Andy then and said, "Very well, we will discuss our business in front of Mr. Adams."

"Thank you, sir."

"Andy, the Corps is prepared to take you and the other men back—as many as will come, that is—with full back pay and no reprisals for leaving."

It was what Andy had been waiting—and hoping—to hear, but he still seemed surprised.

"That's very generous, sir," Andy said. "Very generous."

"Yes, it is," Macleod agreed. "And I don't mind telling you it took a lot of talking on my part to arrange it, but there it is. Tell that to the men and let me know how many are willing to come back."

"I will, sir, I surely will," Andy said.

"Good. Now that's settled, there's another matter to discuss," Macleod said.

"What is that?" Andy asked, frowning.

"The only way I was able to get a payroll for you men was to agree to come and pick it up myself."

"Here?" Andy asked.

"Yes, here, in the Bank of Helena," the commissioner answered. "However, I was only able to free Potts and three other men to come with me."

He hesitated right there and looked over at me. What he was going to say next he didn't really want to say in front of me.

"Mr. Adams," he said—I was surprised that he was addressing himself to me and not Andy—"I want you to know that I recognized your name yesterday when you introduced yourself to me."

"You did?" Andy said, looking puzzled.

"I know who you are," Macleod went on. "And I know that, as an ex-lawman, I can trust your discretion."

"Commissioner, I'll leave the room if you like—" I started to say, but he cut me off.

"There's no need for that, I assure you," he said. "I need only your word that nothing I say will go outside of this room."

"You have my word," I said.

"Andy, there's a condition involved in our offer to take the men back."

"What condition?"

"Well, it's not a difficult one to meet," he said. "Any man who rides back with me, as escort to the payroll I'm here to pick up, will be accepted back under the previous conditions I have outlined."

"I don't think that will be a problem, sir," Andy said. "We have to go back anyway; we might as well ride back with you."

"Good," he said, "very good."

Andy stood up as if to leave, but there was still a question I thought should be answered.

"Commissioner, I don't know if I have the

right to ask this question," I said, also standing.

Macleod looked at me and stood up himself.

"Your presence here gives you the right," he assured me.

"How much of a payroll are we talking about?" I asked.

From the expression on Andy's face, I knew that the answer interested him as well.

"A big one," he answered. "Big enough for me to worry about bringing it back with only five men, or even ten."

"How big?" I asked.

He looked at both of us, then took a deep breath and said, "Fifty thousand dollars."

THIRTY-THREE

"No wonder he wants you guys back," I said to Andy. It was later, at Jake's, and we were having a beer.

"You think all he wants is an escort back to Canada?" he asked. "And once he gets us there he'll arrest us for desertion?"

"I didn't say that. The fact that he got himself a payroll means he wants to pay the men, but which men? The ones who left, or the ones who stayed?" I didn't mean to plant a seed of doubt in his mind, but there was already some growing in mine. "You know the man better than I do, though," I went on, "and we've already established that I'm a pretty suspicious person."

"Fifty thousand dollars," he said, as if he hadn't even heard the last thing I said. "That is quite a lot of money."

"Especially considering he's got to transport it three hundred miles from here to Canada," I pointed out further.

"Yes," he agreed. "That could be his primary concern, getting the money back safely."

"I guess you'll just have to explain his proposal to the rest of the men and let them make up their own minds," I said.

"That would seem best," he said, staring into his beer and swirling it around in the glass.

"And I think it would be better if you simply presented it to them without voicing any of your own—or my—doubts," I said.

"Yes," he said, still staring into his drink.

"Hey," I said, nudging his arm. "What are you thinking about?"

He started when I nudged him, then said, "Oh, I was just thinking . . . this was what I wanted to happen, and now . . ."

"And now I've made you think twice," I said, "and doubt a man you've obviously trusted."

"No, no, that's not it," he said hastily. "Don't blame yourself for anything. I would have sat down and thought twice about it myself, and so will the others. If we do go back and are arrested, it won't mean that the commissioner knew anything about it. He could be acting in good faith."

I felt bad about having said anything and wished I could take the words back.

"When will you tell them?" I asked.

"I will ask Jake if he will give us the back room again this evening, for another meeting," he said. "Will you come?"

"If you want me to."

"Yes, I do," he said. "You were there with me, so you should come to the meeting. If the men ask us for our reactions I think we should be honest with them," he said.

I was about to apologize for that, but decided that wasn't the thing to do, so instead I said, "All right, whatever you say."

"There is something I want to ask you about," he said then, "but I think I will get two more beers first."

"All right."

I knew what he was going to ask me. Commissioner Macleod had been a lawman for a long time, and it figured that he would recognize my name, and now it was only natural for Andy to be curious about it.

When he came back with the two beers and sat back down I said, "You're wondering why Macleod recognized my name, right?"

"Right," he said with a short nod. "We have never spoken of your past, and I have never asked, but now my curiosity is aroused."

"Can't say that I blame you," I said. "Truth of the matter is, I have a reputation that I don't go around talking about. I was a lawman in various parts of the Southwest for about eighteen years . . . and I built up a reputation, I think, as a good lawman."

"And that is why Commissioner Macleod recognized your name, from your reputation as a lawman," he finished for me.

"Well, I hope so," I said, and he frowned.

"What do you mean, you hope so?"

"Along the way," I began, "I also acquired—no, I guess that's not right. I guess I 'earned' myself another reputation. With a gun."

"You are a gunfighter?" he asked.

"I always thought of myself as a lawman who happened to be good with a gun," I said. "But people, and newspapers, had a habit of looking at it differently."

"How?" he asked.

"Well, the newspapers especially got a hold of it and, early in my career, they started calling me the Gunsmith, because I usually make and repair my own guns."

"And you are very good with guns?" he asked.

"Uh, yes, I am," I admitted. "It's a skill that seemed to come very naturally to me as a young man."

"So, you *are* a gunfighter?" he asked, and I could see the excited look in his eyes. He was meeting a *real* gunfighter!

"That's the way most people react," I said.

"What?"

"Just the way you are," I said. "I'm not Wild Bill Hickok, or Jesse James, or John Wesley Hardin. I'm not anybody like that at all."

"Oh," he said, looking kind of disappointed.

"I didn't think my reputation had come this far north," I said.

"But it has."

"Well, I was thinking about that a little bit," I said. "Macleod recognized my name because he's a good lawman, but I was thinking—what if some-one else in town also recognized it? What if that was why somebody shot at me the other night?"

"You mean, they were trying to get a reputation by killing you?" he asked.

"Well, that's the way it sometimes works," I admitted. "But you can't gain much of a reputa-tion by shooting someone from ambush."

"No, that doesn't make much sense," he agreed. "Have you any reason to believe that someone may have recognized you?"

"None," I said. "I've thought it over. I've gotten in the habit of watching people's faces closely when I introduce myself, and I can usually tell if my name means anything to them. I haven't gotten that impression from anyone."

It occurred to me that my argument really didn't mean all that much, because Macleod had obviously recognized my name, but I hadn't sensed it in him at the time. Still, under normal conditions, I had become fairly good at reading people's faces when they heard my name.

"Well, I better start talking to the other men," Andy said, finishing off his second beer. "I asked Jake about it when I got these two drinks, and he said it was all right, so I'll see you tonight, at about eight o'clock, all right?"

"Sure, I'll be here," I said.

When he left I nursed the remainder of my beer, trying to figure out my next move. The only thing I could come up with was going back over my steps since arriving in Helena, talking again to all of the people I had met.

I decided to start with Abby O'Shea.

THIRTY-FOUR

I went over to Abby's and found the place empty, as usual—and that meant no customers, and no Abby. I was about to call out to her when I thought better of it. She spent an awful lot of time in that back room, and I thought that maybe I would just go back there and find out why.

I walked around behind the counter and listened at the curtain for a few moments. I heard a familiar sound, but I couldn't be sure what it was without looking.

I parted the curtain, and there was Abby O'Shea, standing in a hole, digging. That was the sound I'd heard. Only she wasn't really in a hole, it was more like a tunnel. To get to it, you had to step down into a hole, and then there was a tunnel about five feet deep and Abby, digging away.

"What the heck is this all about?" I asked.

She turned violently at the sound of my voice, holding the shovel out in front of her like a spear.

"What the hell are you doing here?"

"That's what I was asking you, only in a nicer way," I said.

"You can't come barging in here," she said. "This is my place—"

"I didn't come barging in anywhere," I said.

"I'm a customer. I came in and nobody was here. I called out, but you obviously didn't hear me, so I came looking for you, and here I find you, standing in a hole."

"It's not a hole," she said, lowering the shovel.

"No, you're right," I said. "It's not. It looks more like a tunnel. Where does it go?"

"It doesn't go anywhere," she said quickly. "It's not a tunnel, it's—uh—it's a root cellar."

"For a root cellar you should be digging down, not straight," I pointed out. "Was this the job you were talking about? You wanted me to dig it for you?"

"No—I mean, yes—"

"But if it was a tunnel," I went on, "where would it be leading to, hmm?"

"Nowhere," she said. "I told you, it's not a tunnel."

I wasn't listening to her denials. I was busy projecting the tunnel to find out where it would lead to, and I could only come up with one logical place. "The Bank of Helena," I said.

She jumped. "What? Don't be ridiculous. The bank?"

"Yes," I said. "The bank. You're digging a tunnel to the bank, and it's not to make a deposit."

"You're being—"

"Little lady, you're planning to rob the Bank of Helena, aren't you?" She just stared at me, her jaw set. "I don't believe it."

"What's to believe?" she said at last, dropping the shovel. "There's a lot of money in that bank, and I can use a lot of money."

"Can't we all? And you're planning on doing this alone?"

"Well, I offered you a job, didn't I?"

"That was the job? Robbing the bank? You'd offer that job to a perfect stranger?"

"I would have cut you in," she assured me.

"But why would you offer that to a man you've just met?" I asked her.

"Because you were a stranger," she said. "You had no money in that bank, as most of the men in this town do, and you had no ties to this town. And you were obviously not a lawman. But," she continued, stepping up out of the hole, "you weren't interested . . . then." She put her hands on her hips and said, "I suppose you're pretty interested now, though, aren't you?"

"Why would I be?"

"There's a lot of money in that bank, Adams. Enough for two people to live very comfortably."

"You and me?" I said, with a leer.

"Separately," she said coldly. "Not together. That is not what I was suggesting."

"Oh," I said, trying to look appropriately disappointed. It was all I could do, actually, to keep from laughing out loud. She was so serious about it, now that she had stopped denying it, that it was comical.

"Well, do you want in?"

"Not if it means I have to do any digging," I said.

"Well, you don't think I'm going to cut you in and then do all the digging, do you?" she demanded.

I sighed audibly and said, "I guess you'll have to let me think about it."

"Well, don't take forever," she said. "I'll keep digging until you make up your mind, but you better let me know by tomorrow."

"Sure," I said. "One way or another, you'll know tomorrow. But tell me what makes you so sure it's worth the effort. The mines don't keep their payrolls in the bank, do they?"

"No," she said. "They pay once a month, and they bring it in from outside under heavy guard."

"Then what makes you—"

"But there is a payroll in the safe now," she said. "It's not for the mines, and I don't know what it's for, but we can't have very much time to get it out. I've already been working almost a week."

"How do you know about it?"

"Never mind," she said. "Just take my word for it. There's over fifty thousand dollars in the bank vault, and I want it."

"How do you intend to get into the vault once you've tunneled into the bank?" I asked.

"I'm not just tunneling into the bank," she said. "I'm tunneling right into the vault itself. The floor is made of dirt and wood."

I'd run into typical efficiency like that when I was wearing a badge. The bank spends money on a strong safe with impenetrable walls and ceiling, and then gives it a wooden floor.

Suddenly, Abby's determination was not so funny. It was obvious that she had access to some kind of inside information, or else how would she have known about the fifty thousand dollar payroll? Given enough time, her plan might work, with or without my help.

I suppose I could have just turned her in, right then and there, but that seemed like a last resort; I'd seen enough of prisons and prison guards in my time to know what a conviction would mean. And I didn't like the thought of turning her over to an incompetent sheriff in a town full of rowdy miners. There was no love lost between me and Abby, but she didn't exactly seem the criminal type—just a little crazy. Maybe I'm just a sucker for a woman alone, but I felt sure I could scotch her plans in some other way.

The best way to stop her was to make sure she didn't have the time she needed.

The payroll had to be moved, and soon.

THIRTY-FIVE

I left Abby in her hole, promising to give her my answer the next day.

"I'm warning you, though, Adams," she said, "if you give me away to the law—"

"For what?" I asked her. "You haven't broken any law yet."

"Just remember I'm determined to get this done, and I won't take kindly to anyone who tries to get in my way."

"I'll remember," I promised, leaving her looking grim and determined—and kind of pretty, with dirt smudges on her right cheek, and the tip of her nose. There was such a fire in her eyes when she talked about money, I wondered what would happen if I could get her that excited about . . . other things.

I had already seen the Sheriff since the shooting, and he had not been very much help. I was almost sure he hadn't recognized my name, anyway. Hell, I'd bet he looked at the shine on his boots more than he ever looked at any wanted posters. He could have Wes Hardin in his town and not know it.

Who else was there? Andy and the other Mounties, but we had already decided that since I was helping them there was no reason for any of them to want me dead.

Of course, there was the gambler Gates, who was supposed to have left town after that first night, but I didn't think he ever had the nerve to shoot at me from ambush. The same went for the dealer at Miss Lottie's.

That left me with Miss Lottie herself, Leticia Newman. She had also offered me a job, although with her it was more likely a job as a dealer. I had been to Miss Lottie's twice, and had never seen Leticia Newman there. That was in the evening, during "business" hours. The one time I had seen her had been early in the morning, at her house. It was afternoon now, but I felt that her house was my best bet of finding her.

On the way to her house I thought more about Abby O'Shea. She had no motive to try and kill me, because she had never explained to me that the job she wanted me for was robbing a bank. If I turned her down, it would give her a motive, which would be to keep me from exposing her, but as far as the shooting which had already taken place, there was no reason to believe she had anything to do with it.

When I reached Leticia's house I knocked on the door and it was answered by the maid.

"I'd like to see Miss Lottie," I told her.

"Do you have an appointment?" she asked.

"No, I don't, but tell her it's Clint Adams, and tell her it's very important."

"You wait here," she said, closing the door and leaving me on the doorstep. She came back a few minutes later, looking very bored, and said, "She'll see you. Come this way."

I followed her and she took me a different route than she had the first time I was there. We came to a closed door, which she opened.

"Mr. Adams, ma'am," she said, and moved aside so I could go in.

I found myself in a large sitting room. Right in the center was Leticia Newman wearing a silk morning gown, seated on a plush divan.

"Middle of the day and you're still not dressed?" I scolded her.

"I am a woman of leisure, Clint," she said. "What was so important that you had to see me?" She looked past me at Lulu and said, "You can leave, and shut the door."

"Yes, ma'am."

"Cute little maid," I commented.

"She was one of my first girls, before I opened Miss Lottie's," she said. "She was one of my most popular girls. When I got successful and bought this house, I took her with me and gave her this job. It's less strenuous for her, and it pays better. Why don't you have a seat?"

"Thank you," I said. I pulled up a chair that matched the divan and found it very comfortable. If I had had any ideas about Leticia Newman having designs on the bank, I put them out of my mind. She had spent more than fifty thousand dollars just buying and furnishing that house.

"Now what's so important?" she asked.

"Somebody took a couple of shots at me a couple of nights ago," I told her.

"How terrible," she said. "I hope you weren't injured?"

"No, but the shots were fired from the roof of the Pleasure Palace."

"Really?" she said. "How odd. You don't think that I had anything to do with it, do you?"

"Not really," I said. "I checked out the roof of your place last night."

"Then you know there are ways to get on and off that roof—any roof—without going through the building."

"Yes, I found that out," I said.

"Are you here to find out if it was me who was shooting at you?" she asked.

"That wasn't my intention," I said, "but if you want to confess—"

"Never mind," she said. "Just get to the reason you came to see me."

"Well, there are several I could think of," I said, and she smiled at that, "but I really came to ask you about that job you offered me."

"You want it?" she asked.

"No," I said. "I still don't want it, but I'd like to know what it was."

"Why?"

"I'm just retracing my steps, Leticia, trying to fill in some blanks. Somebody shot at me and I don't know why. I'd like to find out."

She stared at me for a few moments, then said, "I guess that makes sense. You made a fool out of one of my dealers. I just thought you might like to replace him."

"That's it?" I asked.

She shrugged and said, "That's it. Did you expect something more sinister?"

"I don't know what to expect," I said. "Yes, I did. I figured you wanted a competent dealer, but maybe I was hoping for something more sinister."

"Sorry to disappoint you," she said.

"What about that dealer of yours?" I asked.

"Taking a shot at you, you mean?" she asked. "I doubt that very much. Randy Loomis has never had anything more lethal than a deck of—"

"—cards in his hands, I know," I said, finishing for her. "I already figured that out."

I stood up and I was surprised when she stood up with me and walked to the door.

"I'm sorry I couldn't be more help to you, Clint," she said, sounding as if she really meant it.

"I didn't really think you could, Leticia," I said, "but thanks for trying. I guess I may just have to wait for whoever it was to make another try."

"You mean, wait for him to shoot at you again?" she asked.

I nodded.

"I'll just have to act a little quicker next time, that's all," I explained.

"Sure," she said. "If he hasn't become a better shot by then."

"He was too bad a shot the first time," I said.

"What do you mean by that?"

We were out in the hall now, walking to the front door.

"He had too clean a shot to miss me the first time, if he was any kind of a marksman," I said.

"And if he wasn't?"

"Then he shouldn't have tried it," I answered.

"So what you're saying is that he missed you on purpose? That he was just trying to scare you? Into what—leaving town?"

"That makes the most sense to me," I said.

"But you're not leaving."

"Not just yet."

She was shaking her head as she opened the front door for me and she said, "Maybe you're not as smart as I thought you were."

THIRTY-SIX

Maybe she was right.

Maybe I was banging my head against a stone wall. I had to admit it was next to impossible to find out who had taken those shots at me, unless whoever it was came up to me and confessed.

Or unless he tried again.

I went to Jake's saloon for the meeting. When Andy came in with Robert, LeClerc and Dan Dupree, we all went into the back room, carrying full mugs of beer.

I asked Andy what he thought the consensus would be.

He shrugged and said, "The men seem to be undecided. Some of them never thought of this happening and need time to think about it."

"What about them?" I asked, indicating his three friends who were sitting down at a table.

"They're undecided, except for Dan. He doesn't want to go back. At least, not until he gets that dark-eyed girl," he said, grinning.

"You're kidding," I said, smiling back.

"No, I'm not," he said. "And neither is he."

A few other men started drifting in and they started banding together, discussing the matter among themselves. I took a seat in a corner with my beer and waited for the meeting to come to order.

When everyone was present I counted heads. There were exactly eighteen men present, and me. I started studying their faces, wondering if one of them had been on that roof for some reason, taking a couple of shots at me.

"Quiet down, please," Andy Beauchamp finally called out.

Everybody got quiet and found a seat and focused their attention on Andy. I stayed in my corner, determined to stay silent unless I was spoken to.

"You all know why we're here," Andy said. "I've spoken to all of you during the course of the day. I am going to ask for a show of hands of those men who are willing to accept the commissioner's offer.

Six men raised their hands, and then Andy added his, making a total of seven.

"How many are in favor of not accepting?" he asked.

Eight men raised their hands.

"Undecided?"

The remaining three men raised their hands. That meant that seven were in favor, and eleven didn't want to go, although three of them could have gone one way or the other.

For the commissioner's purpose of guarding the payroll, he had an additional seven men, giving him twelve.

Not enough for fifty thousand dollars. He'd need at least eight more before he could feel reasonably confident.

"I guess we should talk about this," Andy said. "If no one objects, I'll go first."

He discussed the reason why he accepted and reasons he could think of for not accepting; what it amounted to was that he had been waiting for this, and he trusted Assistant Commissioner James Macleod.

Several other men spoke up and gave their views. The consensus of opinion of the men who didn't want to accept was that the Corps simply wanted to lure them back in order to arrest them.

"We can check the bank and see if the money is really there," Robert spoke up.

"I'm not saying there is no payroll," another man said. "I'm just saying that it's part of the plan to get us back so they can arrest us."

"Why would they be so concerned about arresting us?" LeClerc asked. "There's only eighteen of us."

"Eighteen this time," the other man said. "If they let us get away with it, there could be eighty next time."

It went back and forth like that for a good long while, and then they took another vote.

Six total for accepting.

Ten for not accepting.

Two undecided.

Instead of getting better, it was getting worse.

"Let us ask our friend, Clint Adams, what he thinks," Dan Dupree suggested, and everyone looked towards me.

I stood up and said, "Not knowing what it's like in the Mounties, or what Commissioner Macleod is like, it would be very difficult for me to advise you. But, since you asked, I think that if this man,

Commissioner Macleod, is the man some of you say he is, then I'd trust him. I'd ride with him to safeguard the payroll and get it delivered to Canada safely." I thought about Abby O'Shea, who knew about the payroll, and I wondered how many others knew. "He may need all of you to get it there safely. And then again, even all of you may not be enough."

THIRTY-SEVEN

The back room was empty now, except for me, Andy, Robert, LeClerc and Dan Dupree.

"What was the last vote again?" I asked.

"Six for, twelve against," Andy answered.

"Well, at least we helped them all make up their minds," I said.

"How do we stand here?" I asked.

I looked around the table and they were all looking at each other.

"Robert and LeClerc voted for," Andy said, "as I did."

"And I vote for, also," Dan Dupree said. He put out a big paw and clamped it down on Andy's shoulder. "You came with me to keep Dupree out of trouble, I go with you for zee same reason."

"And there were two others," Andy said. "Boyer and Gilbert."

"Six men," I said, "combined with Macleod and his four. That makes eleven to escort the payroll back. I shook my head and said, "I don't think that's going to be enough."

"Why not?" he asked.

I told him that Abby O'Shea knew about the payroll and was trying to dig her way into the vault.

"What?" Andy said.

"The woman is crazy," Dan Dupree said.

"Maybe so," I said, "but given enough time, she'll make it into the vault. With luck, however, the payroll will be gone by then. You'll all have left with it already. What I'm getting at, though, is that if she knows, somebody else could know."

"Who?" Andy asked.

"I don't know," I said. "I'm simply saying *somebody* could. That someone may not be thinking about getting the money from the vault. He may be waiting for someone to try to transport it."

"You mean that someone is sitting out there waiting to steal it from the Commissioner?" Andy asked.

"I'm saying it could be," I corrected him.

"Eleven men," Andy said.

"Do not worry," Dan Dupree said. "With Dupree, it is like having fifteen."

"Six?" Macleod said.

It was the next morning and we were in the commissioner's hotel room with the news of how many men were willing to go back.

"That's all," I said.

Andy had agreed not to say anything about Abby O'Shea, and I was wondering how I could arrange to be inside that vault when she finally broke through and found it nearly empty.

"That is disturbing," the commissioner said.

"Eleven men," Jerry Potts said. "If we were to be set upon by thieves, Commissioner, we would only be eleven men."

"Twelve," I said.

"I beg your pardon?" Macleod said, looking at

me. "Did we miscount somewhere?"

"No, sir," I said. "My friend, Andy, here has convinced me that I should see Canada before I head south again. That is, if you will have me, sir."

Potts gave Macleod a quick look, which the commissioner pointedly ignored.

"Of course we'd like to have you, Mr. Adams," he said to me. "I think that was a good suggestion by Andy."

"Thank you, sir," Andy said.

"I think we should leave as soon as possible," I suggested to Macleod.

"I agree," he said. "I have made arrangements with the bank to have the money ready for transport at a moment's notice. How soon can you and the other men be ready?"

I nodded to Andy and he said, "At any time, sir."

"Good," Macleod said. "We'll leave in the morning, at daybreak."

"Fine," Andy said. "I'll let them know."

As Potts showed us to the door, Macleod called out Andy's name.

"Yes, sir."

"I know you tried your best, Andy," Macleod told him. "I appreciate that. And I appreciate your help, Mr. Adams."

"I always wanted to see Canada, anyway," I told him.

"It's a beautiful country," Macleod said.

When we got out into the hall Andy stopped me and said, "It's a beautiful country, all right—but you've got to know where to look."

I tapped him on the chest and said, "You show me. Come on, we have a lot to do."

Andy reported to his fellow-Mounties, and they collected their pay, made good on debts, and wapped up their affairs—business and otherwise. I spent the best part of the day laying in supplies for the trip. I made a point of not giving my business to Abby, figuring the less she knew, and the later she knew it, the better.

THIRTY-EIGHT

I woke up the next morning at first light. I dressed as warmly as I could, strapped on my gun, and then grabbed my saddlebags, rifle and supplies, and went to the livery to get Duke.

I made arrangements with the liveryman to take care of my rig and team, and then went to saddle Duke up myself.

"How you been doing, old boy?" I asked him. I swear that horse looked at me and frowned, as if he was trying to remember who I was.

"I know, I know," I said. "I've been neglecting you, and I'm sorry, but we're going for a long ride now." I got him saddled up and then weighed him down with the supplies. I rubbed his nose and patted his neck and said, "I know you're annoyed with me, but you're going to get plenty of exercise where we're going, and pretty soon you might be wishing you were right back here again."

He shook his great big head like he was telling me he doubted that very much, but I said, "You shake your head at me like that a week from now, pal."

I backed him up and then mounted up. It felt good to be in the saddle again.

Yeah, I told myself, *you tell me that a week from now.*

On the way out I told the liveryman, "With a little luck I should be back in two weeks."

"And without luck?"

"Don't you worry about that," I said. "Whenever I get back, that rig and team and everything that goes with it better still be here, or I'll pay you off in lead instead of dollars."

"Don't worry, mister," he said, hastily. "Everything'll be just where you left it."

I trotted Duke out into the street and he cantered around like a young colt just getting his legs under him.

"Save that energy, big boy," I told him. "We're going to need it."

I took a tight rein on him and walked him the rest of the way to the bank. It looked like we were about the last to arrive.

" 'Morning, Andy," I said, pulling up alongside of him and the big bay colt he was riding.

"My God, that's a beautiful animal," he said, feasting his eyes on Duke.

"Thanks," I said. Robert, LeClerc, and Dan Dupree were mounted up and ready to go; Jerry Potts was on the ground, holding the reins of a bunch of horses. At that point, Macleod and five men—including Boyer and Gilbert—came out of the bank. Macleod and his three men were all carrying saddlebags, and they all threw them over their horses and mounted up.

Boyer and Gilbert were empty-handed, except for their guns, which they holstered, and then they mounted up as well.

"Are we all here?" Macleod asked.

"Which one of them has the money?" I asked Andy.

"Knowing the commissioner," he said, "it could be one, or all of them."

"Let's move out," Jerry Potts said, mounting up and leading the way.

Twelve men riding out of town was a little obvious, especially leaving from directly in front of the bank. It could have been planned better, but then I was just along for the ride.

First chance I got, though, I was going to find out exactly where that fifty thousand dollar payroll was. I wasn't going to ride all the way to Canada in the dark, that much was for sure.

THIRTY-NINE

According to Potts, the halfway point would be the Metis Pass, through the Rockies—if we made it that far.

"What are you looking for?" Andy asked me.

We were riding at the tail end of the pack and I hadn't realized that I was being that obvious.

"I've got an itch," I told him.

"You are expecting someone to try and take the money from us, aren't you?"

"Yes," I said. "I just hope we have enough men to keep it from happening."

We rode along in silence for a while and I said, "What was it that Macleod said about a border patrol?"

"He said they were stopped by a border patrol of United States Troopers about fifty miles outside of Helena and had to identify themselves."

"Fifty miles?" I asked.

"That was what he said. Why?"

"Fifty miles from Helena, that's about— what—two hundred miles from the border?"

"More like two hundred and fifty," he corrected me.

"Still, fifty miles from Helena, that's a little far

off the beaten path for a border patrol, don't you think?"

"Now that you mention it," he said, "I suppose it is."

"What were they doing that close to Helena?" I wondered aloud.

"If someone is planning to try and steal the money from us, when do you think they would strike?"

"I don't know," I said, shrugging my shoulders. "I guess it would depend on who it was."

"Meaning what?"

"If they're American, I don't think they'll want to be too close to Canada when they hit us," I said. "And if they're Canadian, the other way around."

"Do you think you should tell the commissioner about this?" Andy asked.

"Oh, I'm sure he's aware of it," I said. "He's been looking around even more than I have. Still, when we stop I guess I'll have a little talk with him."

It was almost dark when Potts finally signaled for us to make camp. We all got busy taking out our own gear and caring for our horses, while one of Macleod's men started a fire and put on some coffee. It looked as if he had been elected to be the cook for the night.

As darkness fell the men seemed to break up into twos or threes. I was standing off to one side with Andy and saw that Macleod was alone, staring out into the darkness, so I excused myself and went over to talk to him.

"Commissioner," I said, announcing my presence.

He looked over at me and said, "Oh, Adams," and then continued to stare into the darkness.

"I guess you feel the same way I do," I said.

He nodded and said, "If you feel that there is someone out there, waiting for us, then yes, I do. I am hoping that perhaps we will meet up with a U.S. border patrol. Maybe we can convince them to escort us as far as the border."

"Yeah, maybe," I said. "Commissioner, since I'm along to help protect the money, do you think maybe you could tell me exactly where it is? I mean, in which saddlebag?"

He continued to stare out at the darkness, then turned his head slowly and looked into my eyes.

"I brought along four men who I know I can trust, Mr. Adams," he said. "They went into the bank vault with me, or at least three of them did. I have told Mr. Potts where the money is, so that means that five of us know. I mean no offense when I say that five would appear to be enough."

"What about the other men?" I asked. "Beauchamp and the others. They're Mounties, aren't they?"

"They will be," he said, "when we get back to Fort Macleod. Right now they are deserters."

"Who were promised no reprisals," I reminded him.

"And I shall keep that promise," he said, "but at the moment there is no real reason for you or them to know the exact location of the payroll. That is, unless you are intending to steal it yourself."

"The thought hadn't entered my mind," I told him.

"I didn't think it had," he said. "Mr. Adams, I don't think I am altogether clear on exactly why you decided to accompany us on our journey."

"Well, I'll tell you the truth, Commissioner," I said, rubbing my jaw. "I'm not all too clear on that myself."

"Really?" he said, looking at me with raised eyebrows. "Would you care to explain that statement to me?"

"Well, I was only in Helena a short time, but during that time somebody took a couple of shots at me."

"I suspect that happens quite often to a man with a reputation like yours, Mr. Adams. Being an ex-officer of the law would be bad enough, I imagine, without being known as a gunman, as well."

"Well, you're right on a couple of points, but whether it happens often or not, a man doesn't get used to being shot at, and when it happens, he generally likes to know who did it and why."

"And were you able to find out?"

"No, not yet," I said. "That's part of the reason I came along on this trip."

"I don't understand."

"The only thing in Helena I was remotely involved in was the . . . uh . . . problem of Andy and his friends."

"You mean, because you agreed to speak on their behalf?" he asked.

"That, and before that, sir. Andy and I had become rather friendly, and he told me about the . . . hardships of being a Mountie, which seemed bad enough to me as it was, without having to go without pay for six months, as well."

"Yes, that was unfortunate," Macleod said. "I tried my best to get some kind of a payroll before now—"

"Andy explained that to me, sir," I said. "He said the men had a lot of respect for you, and I think I can see why."

"Well, thank you very much for that, Mr. Adams," he said. "However, I still don't feel obligated to treat them as full-fledged Mounties until we have reached Canada and Fort Macleod safely."

"Well, I guess I can see your point, sir," I said.

"And I believe I can see yours, as well," he said. "Since this was all you were involved in, you thought to come along and . . . just see what happened?"

"That's right."

"Well, I would hate to think it was one of these men who shot at you," he said, "but I hope you find a satisfactory answer to your dilemma."

"So do I, Commissioner, so do I."

He went back to staring out into the darkness, and I was sure that his ears were just as wide open as his eyes.

I went back to sit by Andy, on the far side of the fire. He had already filled a tin plate with food for me, and I took it from him.

"Beans," he said, "bacon and bread."

"Coffee?" I asked, hugging myself against the chill in the air.

"Hot, too," he said, handing me a cup.

I put down my plate and let the coffee warm my hands, then I took a sip and enjoyed the way it warmed my insides. After that I started in on my dinner.

"Did he tell you where the money was?" he asked.

"No," I answered around a mouthful of beans. "He didn't see the necessity of telling me . . . or you, for that matter."

"He doesn't trust us?" he asked.

"Would you trust five men who had deserted, and one who had a reputation with a gun?"

He thought it over for a moment, then shrugged and said, "No, I can't say that I would."

FORTY

It was cold, colder than it had been in Helena, and I wondered how much colder it would get when we started getting close to the Rockies, and Metis Pass.

"Tell me about the Metis," I said to Andy during the second day. "It'll keep my mind off the cold."

"You think this is cold?" he asked.

I stared at him. "The Metis. I know they're Indians—"

"Well, they are not Indians, but neither are they white. They are halfbreeds, and some of them are even of French extraction."

"Is that so?"

"There have been Metis in Canada since the sixteen-fifties," he went on. "Descendants of Champlain's men."

He told me they were individualists, and dressed half white, half Indian. They elected a leader they would call "messiah", who they would obey always.

"Sound like very unusual people," I said.

"Oh, that they are," he agreed.

176

"I figure we've gone about sixty miles, wouldn't you say? Looks like we're beyond the point where Macleod and his men met up with the border patrol," I said.

"Perhaps the border patrol is now much closer to the border," Andy suggested.

"I hope so," I said. "I'd much rather not run into anybody at all this whole trip."

We rode in silence for a few more miles and I tried keeping my mind on something other than how cold I was feeling. I thought about how warm it had been in bed with Abby—who was a cold woman at heart—and with Leticia Newman, and with the dark-eyed whore, Diane. I thought about how nice it would be to be that warm again.

It took a second or two before I realized that our little column had stopped moving.

"What's the matter?" I asked Andy.

"I don't know."

"Well, let's find out," I said.

I rode up on Macleod and Potts, who had their heads together, and asked, "What's the hold up?"

Macleod looked at me and said, "Mr. Potts was just pointing out to me that we had to go through a pass that was a perfect place for an ambush, Mr. Adams. What do you think?"

He inclined his head ahead of us to show me where the pass was, and I gave it a look. All I could see was the mouth of the pass, but it looked pretty narrow to me.

"Does it get any wider as it goes along?" I asked Potts.

He stared at me and then said, "Not so's you'd notice."

"Well then, I'd say he was right, Commissioner," I said. "That pass would be a dandy place for an ambush."

"I agree. What is the alternative, Mr. Potts?" he asked the scout.

"Well, we ain't at the base of the Rockies yet, but this mountain here is still big enough to take two days to go around."

"We've been away too long already," Macleod said. He sat there, tall in the saddle, with his back straight as the back of a wooden chair, staring at the mouth of that pass, trying to make up his mind. "Too long," he said again.

He looked at me, and then at Potts, and said, "We'll go through." He looked at the pass, then nodded at us and said again, "We will go through."

"Yes, sir," Potts said.

"You're calling the shots, Commissioner," I said.

I wheeled Duke around to ride back to the rear of our small troop, hoping that once we rode through, we'd come out the other side . . . alive.

FORTY-ONE

The pass was only wide enough for us to ride through two abreast. Macleod, Potts and the others must have come through safely on their way to Helena, but then they weren't carrying fifty thousand dollars with them.

"We'll go through last," I told Andy.

"All right," he agreed.

We watched as the others rode into the pass, and then finally we followed. As Andy and I entered the pass, I became aware of hoofbeats behind us. I turned in my saddle and saw five men in U.S. Army uniforms riding into the pass behind us.

"Andy—" I said, and he turned and looked as well. They did not have their guns drawn, and there didn't seem to be anything unusual about them.

Suddenly, I heard a shot and wheeled around in my saddle in time to see one of Macleod's three Mounties thrown from his saddle by the impact of a bullet. When I turned back to look at the soldiers behind us, they had their guns out and trained on us.

"Just don't move," the man in the lead said.

The two stripes on his arm told me he was a corporal. "Face front."

I turned and, further up, could see that we'd been stopped by five soldiers in the front, who were also holding guns on us. The man in the lead there was a sergeant.

"What's the meaning of this?" I heard Macleod ask.

"Just do as I say, Commissioner," the sergeant said, "and nobody will get hurt."

"You've killed one of my men already," Macleod said angrily.

"That was just to get your attention, Commissioner," the sergeant said, and then he pointed up to the top of the pass. We all looked up and saw that the walls of the pass were peppered with men holding rifles trained on us. As far as I could see, there were about five men on each side of the pass, which made twenty altogether.

"Now, Commissioner, I'd like your men to close quarters. You can fit three across if you try real hard."

Macleod hesitated a moment, then said, "Do as he says."

With some difficulty, we closed quarters as ordered until we were three abreast, and in that position it was virtually impossible for any of us to get to our guns with any kind of speed. We were practically shoulder to shoulder.

"That's real good, Commissioner," the sergeant said, smiling. I was closer now, and could see that he was a thick-bodied man in his late thirties.

"Now I want your men to take their guns from

their holsters real slow like, hold them over their heads and empty them onto the ground. Oh yeah, if anyone gets any bright ideas, my men are pretty trigger happy, and it's possible none of you would survive. Understand?"

We understood, and none of us was in a hurry to die in that pass. I took out my gun, held it over my head and allowed all of the bullets to fall to the ground. The others were doing the same thing.

"Now you can put them away," the sergeant said. "Since we're closer to the way you came into the pass, I think maybe we'll back out the way you came . . . slow."

So we did that, bumping into each other, everyone aware that one false move could be the last for all of us.

They backed us out of that pass, then bunched us so that we were still pretty much on top of one another.

"What is the meaning of all this?" Macleod demanded at one point.

"I can't tell you that right now, Mr. Commissioner, because we don't have time. Right now, one of my friends is going to come around with a sack, and I want you all to throw your guns in, rifles and handguns. Do it now."

I was beginning to wonder if these men were really soldiers, or if there weren't twenty dead U.S. soldiers lying around somewhere.

A man dressed as a private came around on foot, collecting guns, and we all contributed. I had another gun in one of my saddlebags, a little Colt New Line that I sometimes wore as a belly gun. I decided not to mention it.

"All right," the sergeant said. "Now that we've got all of that out of the way, it's time for us to go for a ride."

The men who had been up on the walls of the pass came down now and walked a ways away to get their horses. If they had tethered their horses closer, we might have heard them before entering the pass. The whole thing seemed to be very well thought out, and I wondered who had done the planning.

"All right," the sergeant said again. "You and your men, Commissioner, are going to come with us, and when we get where we're going, we are gonna talk money."

"I don't know what you are referring to," Macleod said, which I thought was a little silly. The money was either all in his saddlebags, or spread out in four saddlebags, but it was there, and it wouldn't take much to find it. There didn't seem any point in lying.

They herded us together like cattle, surrounded us like drovers, and that was the way we rode off, with the "sergeant" in the lead.

I wondered what Macleod thought of his decision to enter the pass, now.

FORTY-TWO

We rode for hours before reaching a very professional looking camp, with several fires going, and quite a few tents. If I didn't know any better, I would have said it was a genuine U.S. Army camp.

Then again, I still didn't know any better.

"Okay, everybody dismount," the sergeant ordered. "Starkey, have somebody take care of their horses."

"I'll do it, Sarge," the corporal replied.

"Okay," the sergeant said. He turned to Macleod and said, "I want you to come to my tent with me. We're gonna talk."

"I would like to bring a couple of men with me, if I may," Macleod said.

"Sure, Commissioner, bring who you like. Let's go."

"Potts. Adams," Macleod called, and I think both Potts and I were surprised that he included me. We followed him and the sergeant to the main tent, with three soldiers behind us. Inside, the sergeant seated himself behind a field desk and we fanned out in front of it, each with an armed soldier behind us.

"My name is Sergeant Ben Corey," the sergeant said.

"Now I recognize you," Macleod snapped. "You were the ones who stopped us on the way to Helena."

"That's right," Corey said, nodding. "I'm flattered that you remember."

"You mean, this is the sergeant who commanded the patrol that stopped you a week ago?" I asked.

"Yes, this is him," Macleod said.

"Then you're genuine," I said.

"I'm what?" Corey said.

"For real," I said. "You're really in the army."

"Oh, sure, I'm in the army," he said, laughing. "We're all in the army, ain't we boys?" he asked the other three soldiers.

"That's right, Sarge," one of them said. "But not for long."

"Yeah, that's right, not for long," Corey said.

"What does that mean?" I asked.

"That means that we're gonna retire pretty soon," he answered.

"How soon?" Potts asked.

"As soon as my corporal gets in here with our retirement fund," Starkey answered, and he and the three soldiers had a good laugh about that one.

As if on cue, the Corporal came in carrying a set of saddlebags, just one set.

"Did you get it?" Corey asked.

"Yeah," the corporal replied. "I got it. It was on his horse," he said, pointing to Macleod.

"Drop it here," Corey said, clearing the desk top. The corporal stepped in front of us and dropped the saddlebags on the desk.

"Okay, Starkey," Corey told him. "Go out and get the men bedded down for the night, and take care of the other prisoners. We'll bring these three out in a few minutes."

"Right, Corey," Starkey said, and went outside.

"Let's see what we have here," Corey said. He opened the saddlebags and stuck his hand into one of them. When it came out he was holding a stack of greenbacks, banded together.

"Is that pretty, or is that pretty?" he asked aloud, staring at the stack of new bills in his hand. He held it up so the other three soldiers could see it and said, "Look at it, boys. This is our retirement."

"Looks real pretty," one of them replied.

"You can't get away with this," Macleod said. "That money is the property of the Northwest Mounted Police."

"It is?" Corey asked, looking at Macleod. "Well then, here, Commissioner," he said, "you take it back."

Macleod stared at him in silent, impotent rage, for he knew there was no way he could get that money back the way things stood right then.

"No, I guess you know you ain't getting this back," Corey said, putting the money back. "Not while me and my boys have it." He looked into the other saddlebag, just to satisfy himself that it held more of the same.

"How can you do this?" Macleod asked, trying another tact. "Have you no loyalty to your uniform, to your country—"

"Of course I do," Corey answered, looking as

if he were insulted at being accused of not being loyal. "If this money belonged to the U.S. Army, I wouldn't be taking it, but it don't belong to the U.S., so I ain't being disloyal to my country by, uh, taking it off your hands."

The frightening thing was that he believed in the logic of what he'd said.

"Besides, you got a long way to go before you get to Canada," he added. "Somebody else was bound to take it off you."

"Can I ask a question?" I said.

Corey frowned at me and said, "You ain't the same as these guys, are you? You're American?"

"That's right," I said. "I was just along for the ride."

"Ah, that's too bad," Corey said, shaking his head. "What was it you wanted to ask."

"How did you know about the money?"

Corey started to laugh then, shaking his head.

"That's kind of a funny story," he said. "I was in Helena not long ago, and I met a lady there who had some information about a lot of money being in the bank. Seems she got the info off some teller who was making moon eyes at her, trying to impress her. Well, me and this gal kind of hit it off, you know, and next thing you know, she's trying to get me to rob the bank." He laughed again at the memory. "Determined little thing she was, too, but I don't go for robbing banks much, so I turned her down."

"Abby O'Shea," I said, and he looked at me, kind of surprised.

"That's her," he said. "She try to recruit you, too?"

"She did," I said, "but I wasn't buying, either. When I left, she was busy trying to tunnel into the vault from the back of her store."

"Is that a fact?" he asked, laughing even louder. "I told you she was determined, didn't I? Hell, if she makes it she's gonna be one disappointed lady, ain't she?"

"That she is."

"And you didn't tell her about taking the payroll out of town?" he asked me.

"Like you said, she'll find out soon enough," I said.

"Mister, you're a man after my own heart," he said. "I wish I could see her face when she gets into that vault." We had to wait for him to stop laughing again before he said to me, "You know, I'm sorry we didn't meet someplace else, you know? We might have been friends."

"I doubt it," I said.

That wiped the smile from his face.

"What's the matter, you too good to be friends with me?" he demanded. He stood up, not waiting for an answer. "All right, take them out," he instructed his men. "Tie them up good and tight."

"Where's your commanding officer?" Macleod demanded.

"What?" Corey said. "My commanding officer? Well, you see, he didn't take to this idea when I laid it out for him. When you showed me your papers, I wondered why some Mounties would be riding to Helena, Montana, and then I remembered the payroll that was there. I put two and two together, and told my C.O. about it. He didn't like the idea."

"So what happened to him?" Macleod asked.

Corey smiled at that question, took a stogie out of his shirt pocket, stuck it in his mouth, and said around it, "He died." He waved his arm to his men and said, "Go on, get them out of here."

FORTY-THREE

We were marched over to where the rest of our party was already sitting on the cold ground, hands tied behind their backs.

"What happened?" Andy asked.

My hands were tied and I was pushed down next to him before I could answer.

"These men have gone into business for themselves, it seems," I said. "They've decided to retire from the army, and use the fifty thousand dollars to do it."

"What?" he asked. "They actually are soldiers?"

"That's what the sergeant said," I replied, "and I believe him."

"This is unbelievable," Macleod said, as he was pushed to the ground next to me. "Preposterous!"

"Save your breath, Commissioner," I told him.

"We must save that payroll," he said.

"How?" I asked.

He opened his mouth to answer, stopped and then said helplessly, "I don't know."

"We're a little helpless right now," I said. "Not to mention outnumbered."

"If only the other men had decided to come with us," he said.

"I don't know how much that would have helped, Commissioner," I said. "We all still would have been in that pass together."

"Please don't remind me," Macleod said, and I wasn't sure whether or not it was an attempt at humor . . . but I seriously doubted it.

"What are they going to do with us?" Andy asked. I had the feeling that the question had originated somewhere down the line and worked its way up to us. I could see Robert, LeClerc, and some of the others straining to hear what we were saying.

"They're going to kill us," I said.

"Oh," Andy said.

"Although, in my case, the sergeant said he wished we could have been friends."

"But he's going to kill you anyway?"

"Oh, yes," I said. "He feels it's absolutely necessary."

"You are taking it very well," Andy said.

"So are you."

"I don't think it's hit me yet," he said. "I am not even back in the Mounties, yet I am going to be killed because I was trying to protect a Mountie payroll."

"I think you better pass the message down," I advised him, "before the rest of them strain their necks."

He looked down the line at the others, and then said, "Why bother?"

I looked down the line and agreed with him. They were thinking the worst, anyway; why confirm it for them?

"I guess I should have stayed in Helena and got shot at," I said to Andy. "At least I'd have been able to shoot back."

"I'm sorry, Clint," he said.

"For what?"

"I talked you into coming along," he said.

"Oh, really?" I said. "I don't recall you twisting my arm, or holding a gun to my head. I make my own decisions, friend, and this one was all mine."

He grinned and said, "Don't blow your top."

"Why not?" I asked. "Should I wait for them to do it for me?"

"How can you joke?" Macleod asked.

"Commissioner, you strike me as a man curiously without any sense of humor at all," I said honestly. "You never joke under normal conditions, so I can see where you wouldn't understand why I'm doing it now."

"I don't understand," he said.

"That's what I just said," I replied, and that only made him look more puzzled. I leaned over to Andy and said in a low voice, "Let's watch for a while."

Activity in the camp was dying down. Apparently, the guards had been set, and the remainder of the men were bedding down for the night. Three men were still moving around, probably the guard, but I recognized all three of them as the men who had been in the tent with Corey. Also, the corporal—Starkey—was moving around, as well.

I smelled a double-cross of some kind.

"What I can't understand," Andy said, "is how they expect to split fifty thousand dollars over twenty ways, and expect it to be worth the effort."

"That'd be less than twenty-five hundred each," I said. "Unless they are easily satisfied, I agree."

And the smell of a double-cross began to get even stronger, because Sergeant Al Corey did not strike me as the kind of man who was very easily satisfied.

FORTY-FOUR

The ground was getting colder and harder by the minute, and my hands were starting to get numb; whether from the cold or from the lack of circulation I didn't know, but I was starting to lose feeling.

"How are your hands?" I asked Andy.

"Numb," he said.

"Mine, too."

"What does it matter?" he asked.

"We've got to try and get each other loose," I said.

"Why? Even if we did, we're outnumbered, and we have no weapons," Andy said.

"I don't think we'll be so outnumbered for long," I said. "And I have a gun in my saddle-bag. I jerked my head towards the horses, who were only a mad dash away. Given the opportunity, I could get to my gun in a couple of seconds. Even in the dark, Duke stood out among the other horses. He was that much bigger than the rest of them.

"All right," Andy said.

We maneuvered around so that we could reach each other's hands, and still not be conspicuous. There wasn't much danger of being discovered, though, because no one was paying particular attention to us. There was something going on, all right, and it was going to come to a head at any moment.

"Hurry," I said. When all hell broke loose, I wanted to be ready.

"I can barely feel the ropes," Andy said from between his teeth.

I could barely feel his, either, and the effort of working on them was starting to make me sweat, which at the same time was making me feel colder than hell.

Suddenly, the flap on Corey's tent was thrown back and he stepped out. Starkey, who had been standing near the tent, looked over at him and they exchanged glances.

"Look," I said.

Starkey then looked over at each of the three guards in turn, nodding to them.

"It's going to happen now," I said, feeling frustrated.

"What is?" Andy asked.

"A double-cross," I said.

As Starkey and Corey eased their guns out of their holsters, and the guards shifted their rifles to the ready position, I realized in horror just what was going to happen.

"Oh, my God," I said.

And then the five men were firing into the bodies of the sleeping soldiers, some of whom died silently, while others died screaming. It was the most horrible, coldblooded act I'd ever witnessed—and I had seen a few in my time.

I looked at Andy and Macleod, who were struck dumb by what they were witnessing.

Starkey and Corey kept thumbing back the hammers of their guns and firing, and then they started to reload hastily while the other three kept emptying their rifles into their sleeping comrades.

The whole thing resembled a storm without rain. The sound of the shots was the thunder, and the muzzle flashes were the lightning.

When the shooting was finished, the silence was deafening. The three soldiers with the rifles exchanged pleased glances, then looked over to Corey and Starkey. The sergeant and the corporal exchanged glances again, and I could see the triple-cross coming. They snapped the cylinders shut on the guns, and then began to fire at the three men, who had nothing to defend themselves with but empty rifles.

They died with looks of shock on their faces.

Corey and Starkey didn't look at each other then, they just snapped the cylinders out on their guns again and reloaded.

It didn't take a genius to figure out who was next.

"Well, now we know what the split is going to be," I said to Andy. "Two ways: twenty-five thousand each."

"Do you really think they'll each be satisfied with that?" he asked.

"No, I don't," I answered, honestly. "I think somewhere down the line one of them is going to get a bullet in the back, and I think they know it, too."

They both walked over to where we were sitting, eleven helpless men waiting to die, but at least we wouldn't have died betrayed.

"This should be interesting," I said as Corey

and Starkey reached us.

"How do you mean?" Corey asked.

"Well, there's eleven of us here," I pointed out.

"So?" Corey asked.

"So that means that one of you will have to fire six times, while the other fires five times," I said. "What do you think will happen then?"

That stopped both of them. They both had their guns in hand, ready to start firing, but what I said made a lot of sense. That last bullet was going to find its way into one of their backs—but which one?

They were sneaking looks at each other when the bullets hit them. They danced around like puppets on a string while bloody holes were punched through their bodies, and then they fell to the ground and remained still.

"Jesus," I said. "What's next?"

FORTY-FIVE

"They're all dead," Macleod whispered, the shock evident in his voice.

"Yeah," I said, "and here we are like sitting ducks. Come on, Andy, work on these ropes."

"I don't think that will be necessary," Andy said, turning himself around so that we couldn't reach each other's hands.

"What are you talking about?" I asked.

"Don't worry, Clint," he said. "We'll be loose soon enough."

There was so much confidence in his voice that I looked at him closely, and I was able to see it in his face, too. He wasn't worried anymore, and I wondered why.

"What's going on?" somebody called out from down the line.

"This is crazy," I heard Dan Dupree yell.

"Maybe not," I said. I was watching Andy, and he was looking out into the darkness, waiting . . . for what?

Or who?

And then I heard them. Horses, more than one, maybe even as many as eight, or ten . . .

"Twelve," Andy said, as if reading my mind.

"Twelve horses, and twelve men."

When they rode into the light of the campfires, I saw how he knew how many there would be. There were twelve, all right—the other twelve Mounties!

"I'll be damned," I said.

"What's the meaning of this?" Macleod said. "I recognize those men. They were from the Fort—"

"That's right, Commissioner," Andy said. "They *were*."

The men began to dismount and as some of them began checking bodies to make sure everyone was dead, three of them came over towards us.

"That was close," Andy said to them. He turned so that they could untie his hands. When he was free he stood up, massaging his wrists and told them, "Untie him," pointing to me, "and the rest who are with us."

"The Commissioner?" one of them asked.

Andy shook his head and said, "Leave him tied."

"Beauchamp!" Macleod shouted, but Andy ignored him and walked away. I watched as he entered the main tent, where the money was.

One of the men leaned over and untied me, and I struggled to my feet, trying to rub life back into my hands.

I watched as they went down the line. Robert, LeClerc and Dan Dupree were left tied, as was Macleod and the men who had come with him from Canada.

One man had been killed in the pass.

That meant that the "rest" were only two men,

Gilbert and Boyer. Their hands were untied and they were helped to their feet. That left seven men tied, and probably still marked for death. I wondered why I wasn't the eighth.

"Clint!" a voice called out. I looked up and saw Andy sticking his head out of the tent. He stuck out an arm as well and waved at me to come over. I did so, still rubbing my wrists. My hands were starting to tingle as the feeling flooded back into them.

"Come on in, Clint," Andy said, holding the flap of the tent open. "You must have a few questions for me."

"I do," I said, stepping past him. "But will you answer them honestly?"

"As best as I can," he promised. He went and sat behind the field desk and said, "Have a seat. I found a bottle of whiskey in here."

He picked up the bottle and said, "Sorry I don't have any glasses."

"The bottle is fine," I said. He handed it to me and I took a healthy pull, trying to drive the chill from my bones.

"Ask your questions," he said.

"You know the one I'm concerned with most," I said. "Did you take those shots at me?"

A small smile touched his mouth fleetingly as he said, "Yes, I did, and as you guessed, I missed you deliberately."

"Why?"

"You guessed that, as well," he said. "I was trying to scare you out of town. I knew I wanted to take that payroll, but I wasn't quite sure when or how. Having a famous lawman and gunman like you in town made me nervous, I admit. I guess I didn't realize how well deserved your reputation was."

"Why'd you ask me to stay and help?" I asked.

"Contingency plan," he said. "If you didn't leave town, I wanted to have you where I could see you."

"And now you have," I said.

"Yes, I have," he said, reaching for the bottle. I passed it to him and he took a deep drink from it.

"How many of you are there, Andy?" I asked. "Fifteen?"

"That's right," he said. "Why?"

"Well, we were discussing how Corey was going to keep his men satisfied, splitting fifty thousand dollars more than twenty ways. It would seem to me that you'd have the same problem, splitting it fifteen ways."

"I'm not splitting it fifteen ways," he said. "I'm not greedy, Clint. Since I set this up, and I convinced the other men to come into it, I'm taking ten thousand dollars off the top, and they are splitting the rest."

"Will they be satisfied with that?"

"Twenty eight hundred dollars each?" he said. "That's more money than any of them has ever seen in one place."

"What about your good friends?" I asked. "Robert, LeClerc, Dupree. Why aren't they in on it?"

"I proposed it to them, as a joke, you understand, and they were properly shocked. I knew then that they wouldn't understand, so I didn't bring it up again."

"What about bringing it up now?" I asked.

"Now?" he asked, smiling. "I'm afraid they would say yes, thinking that it would save their lives."

"And would it?" I asked.

He was in the act of tipping the bottle up and stopped, staring at me over it.

"Oh, I'm not going to kill them, Clint," he said. "Just as I have no intentions of killing you."

"What do you intend to do with us, then?" I asked.

"Leave you here," he said. "We will pack up what we need and leave, eventually splitting up and going our separate ways."

"And you'll leave us here to die," I said. "That's not killing us?"

"Well, I won't kill you," he reasoned. "The cold might, but that will be up to yourselves, won't it?"

"How did you get the others to go along with you on this?" I asked.

"Oh, that wasn't hard," he said. "They have always looked to me as a kind of leader."

"Oh, really?" I asked, reaching for the bottle. "Does that mean that you convinced them to desert with you, too?"

"You are a smart man, Clint," he said. "For a while I wondered if I would be able to interest you in a share of fifty thousand dollars, but when I thought about it more, I became convinced that you would never agree. Was I right?"

I took a swig from the bottle and passed it back.

"You know you are," I said. "Are you going to leave us here tied up, to die in the cold?"

"Now what kind of a man do you think I am?" he asked. "I won't leave you tied."

"But you will leave us on foot," I said.

"Clint, I don't want anybody coming after me, for revenge or the money."

"Do you think that Robert, LeClerc and Dupree care enough to go after you?"

"Perhaps not, but the commissioner would," he said, "and I think there's a good chance that you would, too. In fact, considering your reputation, I would probably be safer killing you."

"That's your decision," I said.

"Yes, it is," he agreed. "I think I'll put you back with the others—spacing you well apart, that is, so that you can't play with each other's ropes. Once we're ready to go, I'll tell you what my decision is."

"I can't wait," I said dryly.

He stood up and came around the desk to walk me out of the tent. Outside he called over one of his men and asked him to tie me up with the others.

"And don't let them sit together," he instructed. "I want a wide space between them."

"How about a blanket?" I asked Andy. You know how I hate the cold."

"I wouldn't want you to get too comfortable," Andy said. "It might make any hardships that were to come . . . harder."

"Your concern is touching," I told him.

FORTY-SIX

They spaced us three feet apart, and I sat with Macleod on my right and Dan Dupree on my left.

"I cannot believe this," Dupree said. "Not of Andy Beauchamp."

"Well, you better believe it," I advised him.

"We must do something," Macleod said from my other side.

"Well, I'm working on that right now," I told him. He gave me a puzzled look, but he couldn't see behind me, where I'd been chafing my ropes against a sharp rock for the past ten minutes. Unfortunately, I'd also been chafing some of the skin off my hands, but that couldn't be helped.

"What is he going to do with us?" Macleod asked.

"He says he's not going to kill us," I explained. "He's just going to leave us out here on foot."

"But that's the same thing as killing us," Macleod said.

"Well, I guess the similarity escapes him," I said.

If there had only been some way to get us all untied, we'd have only been outnumbered two to one. There were fifteen of them and eight of us. Even without guns, we'd've at least had a fighting chance.

"Psst," I heard from my left. It was Dupree, leaning towards me as far as he could.

"Have you loosened your bonds yet?" he asked in a low voice.

He must have noticed what I was doing behind my back. I only hoped that no one else had.

I shook my head and whispered, "I'm trying my best."

"Well, hurry," he said. He looked around and when he was sure no one was watching him, he took his left hand out from behind his back to show me that his hands were free. "I am itching for some action."

If Dupree was free, I wondered if the others were, as well. From the way the rope of his left wrist had looked, he'd snapped it with his brute strength. The others would have to do it the way I was, but maybe they'd had a head start on me.

I began to rub my ropes against the rock with renewed vigor. If I could get free and get to my saddlebag, I'd have a gun and be able to do some damage.

"Be patient," I told him.

He nodded, and put his hand behind his back again.

Andy and his men were looking through the supplies of the dead soldiers, taking what they could use and disregarding the rest. They were careful to take all the guns, however, not wanting to leave any behind for us when they left.

That is, if Andy didn't decide to just go ahead

and kill us, just to be on the safe side.

I could feel Dan Dupree's eyes on me, waiting impatiently for me to call the shots. I looked over at Macleod, whose head was down, chin on his chest, the picture of dejection. From what I could see, he was making no effort whatsoever to get loose from his bonds.

Suddenly, with a start, my hands came free and I lurched forward momentarily. I looked up, hoping no one had noticed, but the majority of the men were still busily rifling the pockets of the dead soldiers.

There were two men supposedly guarding us, armed with rifles, but they were also watching the activity in the camp, probably angry because they were missing out on the easy pickings.

I checked Duke again, to make sure that no one had moved him, and I was still close enough to him to reach him in a few strides. The saddlebag that was holding my Colt New Line was on the nearest side to me, so I wouldn't have to reach over his back to get to it. My rifle had been removed from its scabbard.

I looked over at Dupree and nodded my head, to let him know I was free. I tried to use my eyes and my head to relay my message to Dupree that I wanted to lure one of the guards over near us. He seemed to get the message, and in a moment he called out to the guard by name.

"Hey, François," he called, and the guard turned and looked at him.

"Ah, *mon ami,* I do not feel so good," he said to the guard. "Please, could you help me."

The guard gave an impatient shrug, looked over

his shoulder at the activity in the camp, then began
to walk over to Dupree. He passed by me on the
way, but I let him go. My job was to get to my gun,
the guard was Dupree's responsibility.

"What's wrong?" the guard asked Dupree, and
the sound of his voice galvanized me into action.

I got my legs under me and sprinted for Duke.
It occurred to me that, with the entire camp
caught flatfooted by my move, I could have very
easily leaped into the saddle and been gone, but
then it *was* just a fleeting thought.

When I moved, the guard turned his head towards me, but had no time to react or cry out. Dan
Dupree's massive hand came up and grabbed him
and then the action was behind me as I ran to
Duke to get my gun.

I reached Duke and tore at my saddlebags to
get them open and suddenly a horrible thought
occurred to me.

I remembered having told Andy that I had a
gun in my saddlebag. If he had remembered, and
had it removed, then I was as good as dead.

I reached into the saddlebag, looking back at
Dupree, who now had the unconscious guard on
the ground. I saw him toss the man over onto his
back and remove his gun from his holster, and then
he pulled a knife from the man's belt.

The other guard saw what was happening just as
my hand touched the gun in my saddlebag. Almost
by pure reflex I pulled the bag from Duke's back,
and as the guard shouted and brought his rifle to
bear on Dupree, I extended the gun in my hand,
bag and all, and fired right through the leather.
The bullet caught the guard in the chest and he
toppled over.

The rest of the men in the camp looked up and saw what was happening. While they went for their guns, Dupree moved over to Jerry Potts and used the guard's knife to cut him loose. He then thrust the handgun at Potts, keeping the guard's rifle for himself.

I pulled my gun from the saddlebag just as Andy came running out of the tent, gun in hand. He looked over at me and I could tell by the look on his face that he had just remembered what I'd told him about the gun in my saddlebag.

I dropped into a squat and squeezed off a shot at one of the other men in the camp, catching him in the shoulder. Andy was trying to draw a bead on me and I rolled away from Duke, to make sure the big horse wasn't struck by a bullet meant for me.

Dupree and Potts were on their feet now, firing away. Beauchamp's men had been so surprised that they'd been slow picking up their guns. Several of them were on the ground, either wounded or dead.

We had an additional advantage over the men in the camp. They had all been close to the campfires, and when the shooting started their eyes were used to the light. They'd had to look out into the darker area where we were, and hadn't been able to pick us out right away.

I saw Robert and LeClerc cutting the rest of the men free, and then they were scrambling around for fallen guns. Surprise was our main weapon, and we made the most of it.

I looked around, searching for Andy, but he was nowhere to be seen. I ran for the tent and went in low, holding my gun out in front of me, but the tent was empty.

There was a slit in the fabric of the tent in the back. Andy Beauchamp was gone . . . and with him the fifty thousand dollars.

FORTY-SEVEN

I didn't waste any time. I went around the desk and through the slit in the tent, into the darkness. If he had been waiting for me out there he could have shot me dead, but that didn't happen.

I knew Andy wouldn't try to get away on foot. That would have been sheer foolishness. He would need a horse, and the only way he could get one was to circle around behind the action in the camp, come up behind the horses and grab one.

I followed the path I felt he would take to reach the horses, very aware of the shooting that was still going on in camp. Wishing I had my regular gun rather than the New Line, I circled the camp until I came within sight of the horses.

Maybe the cold had numbed my brain, but whatever the reason, the fact remains that I got careless, and it could have cost me my life.

I rushed into the midst of the horses, looking to see if Andy was among them, but he answered that question when he said from behind me, "Drop the gun, Clint."

I stopped short and my grip on the gun tightened, but he said, "Don't make me kill you, Clint. Drop it."

I loosened my grip on the New Line, then let it drop to the ground.

"You can turn around," he said, and I did. He had come from behind an outcropping of rocks, where he had obviously been waiting to see if anyone was following him.

"I figured if anyone followed me it would be you," he said, holding his gun on me.

"Why not just shoot me and be done with it?" I asked.

"I told you before, Clint, I don't want to kill you," Andy said. "But if I did, I surely would not shoot you in the back."

"I'm glad to hear it," I said.

He had the saddlebags with the money thrown over his left shoulder, and was holding his gun in his right hand.

"I should thank you for this," he said to me then.

"For what?"

"For starting this uprising," he said, referring to the shooting in camp. "Now I can get away with the entire fifty thousand without having to split it with anyone."

"But you were planning to do that anyway, weren't you?" I asked.

"I hadn't figured out a way yet," he admitted, "but I guess you were right. It is very hard to be satisfied with a piece, when you can have it all."

He began to move to his right, towards the horses.

"Just move to your left, Clint. I am going to pick out the best horse I can and get going."

"You're not afraid of being followed?" I asked.

"I'll be followed for a while, I'm sure," he said, "but with a good horse under me I'll be able to put some ground between myself and the Commissioner . . . or you . . . or whoever it is who will come after me. I have a few places I can go, Clint, and I don't think I have to worry about being found." He patted the saddlebags and added, "Fifty thousand dollars can take me a long way."

He squared his shoulders and said, "Now back away while I pick out a horse."

He moved in among the horses while keeping an eye on me, and he didn't have to look very far to find the one he liked.

"I've been admiring this horse of yours throughout the whole trip, Clint," he said.

"That's not a good idea, Andy," I said.

"Taking your horse?" he said. "Why not?"

"Because if you take him, you better kill me right now, because I'll be on your trail forever."

"But look at the horse I'll have," he replied. "How would you catch me?"

"On foot, if I have to," I answered, "but I'll find you, and I'll get my horse back. You can have the goddamned money for all I care, but leave my horse."

"I'm sorry, Clint," he said, "but I need the best horse out of the bunch."

Shaking my head I said, "He'll never let you stay on his back, anyway. He won't let anybody ride him but me."

"That's nonsense," he said. "You don't really expect me to believe that, do you?"

He took the saddlebags off his shoulder and dropped them onto Duke's back. The big horse's ears pricked up, but that was the only sign he gave that anything was amiss.

"You may be right about one thing, though," Andy said as he prepared to mount. "It might be a better idea just to kill you now, even though I like you."

"Do it before you mount up, Andy," I said, "I'm warning you."

He smiled, put his foot in the stirrup, and hoisted himself up onto Duke's back.

"See?" he said proudly. He brought his gun to bear on me and said, "I'm sorry, Clint."

He moved Duke's reins a bit, to bring him around so he wouldn't have to fire at me over the big horse's neck, and when he did that I backed away quickly.

Duke spun around much faster than Andy had intended him to, but it only took a moment for Andy to realize that he had no control over the horse at all.

As Duke reared up on his hind legs, the gun went flying from Andy's hand as he looked for something to grab a hold of to keep from being thrown off. He almost succeeded, except that Duke then went up on his front legs and, like a whip, he snapped Andy Beauchamp off of his back high into the air.

I had anticipated Duke throwing Andy, and was bending down to pick up my gun so I'd be able to hold it on him, but I hadn't anticipated what happened next.

I watched as Andy flew through the air and then crashed into a rock wall with such force that his body almost folded in half. He bounced off the wall and fell to the ground, where he lay motionless.

I walked to Duke first and touched his neck.

"Okay, big fella, calm down. It's all over."

And it was. I didn't hear anymore shooting from inside the camp, and when I heard footsteps behind me I turned and saw Dan Dupree coming up on me, bleeding from a gash in his forehead, but grinning nevertheless.

"Finished!" he said, proudly. "You and me, we make good team."

"We sure do, Dan," I said.

"Where is Andy?" he said. "I like to break his back."

"I don't think you'll have to," I said.

I walked over to where Andy was lying on his side, with Dan right behind. When I turned him over I saw blood coming from his nose and mouth, and it was obvious that his neck was broken.

"He's already dead," I said to Dan.

"Good thing for him, too," Dupree said, but I could tell from the look on his face that, as angry as he was, he was also feeling some grief for a man who had been his friend, until he decided that money was more important than friends.

EPILOGUE

Only three men had been killed, and they were
Andy Beauchamp's men. Several others were
wounded, and along with Dupree's injured head,
LeClerc had taken a bullet in the arm.

The amazing thing was that, through the whole
thing, Commissioner Macleod had remained tied
up. Nobody had thought to untie him, or nobody
had the time, but as soon as he was untied, he was
back in control.

"There has been too much bloodshed," he an-
nounced. He offered all of the men who had been
with Beauchamp a chance to come back with him
and become Mounties again, and without Andy
Beauchamp to influence them, they all agreed.

"What about you?" Dan Dupree asked me later. "Would you still like to see Canada?"

"I think I'd like to go back to Helena, collect
my rig, and then keep on going south," I said.
"I've had enough of the cold."

"You are good man," he said, pounding me on
the back, "but you have thin skin. You would never make good Mountie."

"And what about you?" I asked.

"I will make good Mountie," he said, "but first

I go back to Helena too, after money is delivered." He leaned forward and said, "After I get dark-eyed girl, I go back to being Mountie."

The way he played cards, I thought, that could take forever.

Winners of the SPUR and WESTERN HERITAGE AWARD

Awarded annually by the Western Writers of America, the Golden Spur is the most prestigious prize a Western novel, or author, can attain.